THE POWER OF WHY

Why 23 Musicians Crafted a Course

GLORY ST. GERMAIN

To Akaxia & Zeeshqun:

Wishing you every
joy & blessing

Love Caroline ♡
&
Tom

COPYRIGHT

DEDICATION

To my mom Rosabel, who taught me the 5 PARTY lessons and the magic of a smile to achieve my dreams of becoming an entrepreneur, and the passion to share these lessons with all those wanting to learn.

To my son David and my daughter Sherry, who taught me about life, relationships, listening, and unconditional love of family support.

And to my husband Ray, for gifting me with his legendary singing voice every day. Thank you for singing and writing "Where's My Lucy" and sharing our amazing beautiful life together.

CONTENTS

1. Lullabies That Linger   1
2. Why Did I Write Microjazz   6
3. If I Can, You Can   10
4. How I Became a Teacher of Teachers   15
5. Why Did I Develop an Adult Intensive Piano   19
   Course That Includes Happy Birthday
6. Following Intuition   23
7. Who Will Rescue the Damsel In Distress   28
8. The Power of a Positive Mental Attitude   32
9. Transformed from Ordinary to Confident Singers   36
10. It's All About My Students   40
11. Why Improvise   44
12. A Course - Of Course   48
13. A Course Creation Journey Around the World   53
14. It's Not What, It's How   57
15. The Muzie Methodology   62
16. Turning Your Disability Into Your Superpower   66
17. The Podcasting Musician   71
18. IRMTNZ Teacher Training Courses   75
19. A Musical Dream Team   81
20. Why I Created "The Universe of Music"   85
21. A New Perspective Made All the Difference   89
22. Enriching A Musical World Through Ebony and   93
    Ivory
23. One Glimmer of Hope Became the Ultimate   98
    Success Story
    Epilogue   103

    Afterword   105
    Acknowledgments   109
    About the Author   111
    Also by Glory St. Germain   113

LULLABIES THAT LINGER

Caren Jensen
United States

MUSIC HAS BEEN A HUGE PART OF MY LIFE. I EXPERIENCED life-threatening physical and emotional abuse, even in my mother's womb. Though abuse of various forms continued, I had a wonderful grandmother who sang me Weidish hymns and lullabies. They calmed my fears and brought me great comfort. I was safe in her arms and music became my therapy.

Until I was six, my music was held tightly like a blanket of safety around me. A music teacher came to my school and I was mesmerized by the beauty of her voice as she stood with outstretched arms inviting us to simply echo her songs. When I heard my own voice for the first time, I was hooked. I knew then that singing would become the voice of my life story. God heard my cries and provided a way for my thoughts and emotions to be heard out loud. The seeds of my future in teaching were sown.

Several gifted and nurturing music teachers introduced me to the piano, flute, and choir which provided the personal motivation I needed to overcome continued abuse not only at home but at school. Practicing piano and flute taught me to persevere through practice until I conquered my assignments and goals. Singing provided context to express my internal emotional struggles in a safe way.

I learned that not all teachers care deeply about their students: not the outwardly gifted students who bubbled with confidence nor the shy and quiet students tormented by unutterably private life situations which they locked inside. I encountered such a teacher in school, a male teacher, in my eighth-grade year. He would rock my world in both positive and negative ways. He first made it clear to my parents that I was just average and not gifted enough to seek a career in music. I was devastated. My one dream, one goal, one gift as I saw it was at risk. I was determined to prove him wrong.

My motto became, "You Watch, You Wait, You'll See"! By the end of the year, he made a public apology followed by the only music award the school had ever given. Another seed was sown, "Prove them all wrong".

I found my way to college and excelled in everything but music theory. Every class I had taken in theory was taught using different methods, leaving me an unassembled tangle of knowledge. No foundational structure had been built, and I didn't know how to ask for help. I think many musicians have experienced such a dilemma. Just average?

I threw myself into performance, spending hours perfecting techniques for performances. My fears would subside when I sang.

A summer spent in Europe singing and studying greatly expanded my vision of life. Music became my way of telling stories through song and encompassing my thoughts and feelings. Scholarship and leadership doors opened for me, but a crushing blow also came. A professor demanded a trade for continued success and opportunities. Because of my abusive history as a young child, I dropped out of college.

Fifteen years later, married and with two children I adored, I auditioned to sing with a college choir - just for fun. The choir director offered me a scholarship and work-study to finish my degree. Five years later, at the age of forty, I finished my B.A. in music at the same time my daughter graduated from high school.

I felt greatly honored to begin teaching music in the schools. I worked with eight hundred students twice a week in classes, while forming school choirs and honor choirs. I was intrigued with the child's voice and gradually worked my way to half-time while founding a nonprofit for young girls and women. I had arrived at that six-year-old goal, teaching, and providing a place of safety for young women. It was a place for both the gifted and those passionate to just find their voices, to be validated, and supported. For twenty years I poured my heart into six choirs, three performances a year, and worldwide travel. Then the chapter ended.

After some rest, refocusing, and many requests, a new chapter began.

I founded a new voice academy focusing not just on classical music, but jazz, pop, and even some country which was a new dream. But a nagging question had remained in the back of my mind for years - would individual voice training for each ensemble member affect the quality of performance outcomes? I asked each member of the new ensemble to study privately with me as an experiment, with no extra charge at first, to see what the effect would be.

I wanted to build individual skill and confidence to see how the overall ensemble would be affected. Each singer would sing a solo during performances as well as sing with their ensemble. To accomplish this, I had to keep my numbers small. They would perform for one another and learn to take and give critique, and to support one another through growth. I shared leadership at performances; each member of the ensemble began to learn how to direct a song. I surrendered the baton and began teaching them to take personal control and responsibility for success. It was bumpy at times but proved to be the right direction for this learning experiment. Ten years have passed, and I still believe deeply in this process.

Incorporated in every lesson and every rehearsal is the study of the body in movement. Each singer is systematically trained to be aware of their bodies and how they perceive them, to discover if their perceived ideas are really true and accurate, and to adjust those perceptions as we explore the truths together. This is called Body Mapping. The systematic and knowledge-based correction of the body map so that musicians move with efficiency to prevent injury.

Now I incorporate Ultimate Music Theory in everything I teach, as well as in private classes and club classes. That pesky subject that plagued my musical life is now becoming mine. I am thrilled.

Why do I teach and why did I create a course? To provide the best environment, materials, technique, and support both through community and private and group instruction that will support their young dreams. No musician should be handi-capped because they haven't learned theory anymore. No singer or instrumentalist should be injured while playing beautiful music. And finally, no aspiring artist should have healthy tech-nique withheld because they are not among the wealthy or the gifted. Everyone who desires should have a seat at the table to learn if they are willing. I must and will continue to provide the open doors for those who care to learn *The Whole Art of the Musical Experience*.

Author Bio:

Caren Jensen is the founder and CEO of Jensen Academy of Vocal Arts operating since January of 2011. Caren is a Certified ABME Teacher and teaches the course *What Every Musician Needs To Know About The Body.* She is passionate about teaching and training singers in the area of Somatics, efficient and effective movement that enhances performance and prevents injury. Caren also teaches Ultimate Music Theory Club Classes.

JensenAcademyofVocalArts.com

WHY DID I WRITE MICROJAZZ

Christopher Norton
UK/Canada

MY MUSICAL LIFE BEGAN WITH AN INNATE LOVE OF MUSIC, particularly classical music, from a very young age. There was no music in my immediate family, so the reasons for that appeared to be nature rather than nurture. My grandmother had a piano and our summer visits to stay with her gave me an opportunity to play. I could play by ear before I had lessons, which began at the age of eight. My mother took me to the local convent and when she was told their slots were filled, she said "can you just hear him play?" A slot was found right away, and I made rapid progress through grade examinations, festivals, and local competitions. I listened voraciously to music at the same time and discovered composers I really liked – in no particular order – Tchaikovsky, Beethoven, Prokofiev, Nielsen, Poulenc, Ravel, Rachmaninoff, Martinu, Szymanowski... and I liked to play piano music by the same composers. So, I explored a very wide repertoire and read all about "my" composers, read books of analysis, bought scores (and lots of LPs) and was very widely read in terms of classical repertoire by the age of fourteen. At that point there was an innovative course for young composers run by our local university, and I signed up and began composing – at the age of fourteen. The pieces I wrote were influenced by the classical music I liked but were quite wide-ranging stylistically from the word go. I did a music degree at the age of sixteen and loved it – analysis, orchestration, transcription, and keyboard harmony. But a major new factor had crept in – I had finally discovered pop music.

A good friend at university (who later became New Zealand's most eminent rock journalist) introduced me to music that was popular in the early 70s – Genesis, Yes, Pink Floyd, Tubular Bells, but also Man, Supertramp, Steely Dan and Frank Zappa. Once again, my interests were wide-ranging and I got to know a huge amount of music, some of it live (I saw Little Feat, Santana, and Roxy Music in New Zealand in the mid-70s.) I also began to explore jazz, helped by a course about jazz harmony run by the principal bassoonist of the New Zealand Symphony, who was also a jazz saxophonist. I was still writing and slowly aspects of popular music such as rock and jazz began to seep into my writing. I also joined a band for the first time and was suddenly in the heady world of chord charts, busked keyboard parts, and improvisation. As commissions appeared I started to explore ways of combining my two interests – classical music and popular music – in my writing. So, just before I left for the UK in 1977, I wrote some pieces which did the thing I have become known for – the sound of popular music, with voicings that you might find in jazz and pop, but with the notational rigour of classical music. I wrote down what I was playing very exactly, with phrasing, articulation and dynamics, pedalling, and fingering all as near as possible to what I was actually playing. But I tried to capture the *grooves* of certain pop and jazz styles at the same time. Once I was in the UK, I was spotted by one of the music lecturers at York University, John Paynter, who recommended me to the educational music editor at Universal Edition (publishers of, among others, Beethoven, and Carl Orff!) My first published books for the international market were all Christmas titles – easy Christmas duets, a book for two-part singers, piano and percussion, and a book of improvisations on carols called *Carol Jazz* (still popular forty years later). The education manager then said to me, "Could you write me a set of graded pieces in popular styles?" I wrote probably forty pieces in a short period of time while playing at the Edinburgh Festival. When my contact emigrated to Canada and the forty pieces sat in a drawer for the next couple of years.

Then I was introduced to the publishing manager at Boosey & Hawkes and when we met the forty graded piano pieces were what really got his attention. And so *Microjazz* was born – named because Mikrosmos was published by the same company. *Microjazz* 1 and 2 came out in 1983 and the rest is history. Millions of sales later, the pieces from those two books are on every examination board in the world and are still as popular with students and teachers as they were nearly forty years ago. And the secret? Good tunes (I hope), but also the authentic sound of the pieces. One professional pianist on an early tour of America said to me, "You write like I play." Also, the notation is incredibly specific and teachers with no background in pop or jazz can look at the scores and know that what is on the page is enough to get started. Later in the 80s midi accompaniments were done to *Microjazz* and eventually backing tracks. The series expanded to all major instruments with piano, and the series runs to hundreds of titles. Interestingly, a pop publisher said to the man who discovered me, "Why would you publish someone no one has ever heard of?" This was a fair enough question but over time a new concept became accepted.

More recently (but still sixteen years ago), *Connections* was created. This was also a set of graded pieces in popular styles but running to eleven volumes from the outset. The same philosophy applied – authentic popular styles allied to very precise notation. But now the presence of backing tracks means that I could use the notated pieces as a jumping-off point for chord playing and vamping, study of voicing, right hand improvisation, and new compositions springing from each piece's *groove*. *Micro-jazz* and *Connections* have established themselves as series or courses that can be taught as straight music, by the score, or they can be used as a springboard for an exploration of a huge range of styles and ultimately to well-rounded (and well-informed) musicians.

Author Bio:

New Zealand-born Christopher Norton became a free-lance composer in 1980. His educational music series, courses and particularly *Microjazz* and *Connections* are a benchmark for educational music worldwide. He now lives in Stratford, Ontario, Canada.

www.facebook.com/christophernortoncomposer

IF I CAN, YOU CAN

Heather Revell
Australia

HER HEAD FELT LIKE AN ELEPHANT WAS SITTING ON IT. SHE was covered in blood. Her body felt like it was pierced with nails. She wondered who could have hammered those in there. Why was she spinning? She could not feel her right arm. Where was it? Was it still there? Sleep.

Awake again. There were razor blades in her shoulder and back. She cried in pain. The light was too bright. Where was she now? She cried in pain and passed out. Awake again. Now shivering uncontrollably. Was she hot? Was she cold? She couldn't make sense of it. Sleep.

She woke to find herself in hospital and medical staff touching her arm and her head, talking about her, asking her questions. X-Rays, CT Scans and MRI were all done. What was all this? Confusion reigned.

It had been a day like any other. Arriving at school and preparing for the junior choir at 9am in the gymnasium. The electric piano was ready to go. The sound system was on and her plan for this session was on the music stand in front of her.

The children began to arrive with their classroom teachers. Everyone was buzzing with excitement for singing with Mrs. Heather. They knew they would be learning a new song today in readiness for the upcoming performance at the campus Music Day. They chatted together and guessed what today's warm-ups might be. And what song would they be learning? They wondered who would have the lead parts for this song.

She welcomed everyone to choir and – nothing.

It's been three years since that near fatal day. It was a freak accident. While I welcomed my junior choir, some boys were moving a large, portable basketball hoop backboard on a steel pole behind me. These are commonplace in gyms. But this one was rogue. The base had not been filled with water or sand to weigh it down. Consequently, when the boys were moving it, they lost control.

It fell on top of me. Knocked me out. Knocked me down to the cold unforgiving gym floor. It landed on top of me. My head was split open, and I don't recall a thing.

During my rehabilitation the following year, I struggled with everyday functions such as walking, talking, thinking and balance. I experienced concussion, lack of concentration, and memory loss whilst experiencing continuous pain all over my body. In addition I had no energy, vertigo, loss of vision, and hearing loss.

I did not resemble a fraction of the person I had been. The vivacious woman with oodles of personality-plus. The light of the party, the 'hostess with the mostess', the organizer, the planner, and the activator. The gardener, the cook, the mother, the grandmother, and the loud and funny, loving woman. I was an energetic and lively full time (and extra) Music Education Specialist on two campuses. Band director, classroom music teacher, private tutor, choir director and all other things musical.

As I slowly regained some normal brain activity and my

memory returned, I became frustrated that I wasn't out there working with my gorgeous students. I mourned my past life. Angry that I couldn't drive and had lost my independence, I was so frustrated, felt hopeless, desperate, depressed, and sad.

How would I live without my music, my students, and my teaching? I wasn't even able to play the piano! Tragic! And I certainly couldn't play the saxophone or clarinet now because blowing just made my head spin more than it already did. Double Tragic!

One of my daughters who lives in Australia, phoned me every couple of days. She affirmed me, encouraged me, and loved me. Her children told me stories about their adventures and gave me lots of virtual hugs and kisses.

She told me what a wonderful woman I was, and how I am an inspirational mother and grandmother, and how much she believed in me. She told me I was an amazing musician and teacher and that my experience, skills, and expertise needed to be shared with others.

At the time, she was expanding her business and venturing to take it online. She had signed up with a coach who specialized in her field of expertise. She shared bits and pieces from her coaching and encouraged me to do one small thing each day to get back 'into the game' via a different route. She shared insights about starting an online business, creating interest, writing courses, freebies, and heaps more. She challenged me to write something, anything, every day. The challenge was to just start writing about any aspect of music, playing an instrument, music theory, teaching young children, or teaching older students. Basically, just get writing.

And so, I did. I attempted to write a little each day. Some days I could think straight and other days it was a bit crooked. I ended up with a folder full of scribblings, writings, course ideas, practical and theory reflections, and anecdotes.

My daughter gave me some homework, which was funny because I was always the bossy mama reminding her to get her homework completed back-in-the-day. I eventually got it done. Sometimes it took a while because I was still coping with the grief of not being with my students every day. I felt sorry for myself. I was angry with myself. I hated my continual headaches. I hated the continual pain in my back, neck, and legs. It often felt like part of me had died. And I believe it did.

But I had to pick myself up daily and do what I could do. I was eventually able to drive and to walk my dogs on the beach again. That was a huge win for me. And, best of all, I was able to teach a few students privately again. Another huge win.

I found an entrepreneur coach and signed up for her course. The coaching, expertise, experience, and encouragement from her course was just what I needed. I pulled out my folder and began editing and reshaping what I had started before with my daughter. Some days it was hard work, and I needed some help with tech, so I hired an assistant to help with all-things-tech and launched my course shortly after.

So, as much as I hated the drastic change that accident brought to my life, I am thankful that I can still feel accomplished as I coach music teachers and students with my anecdotal and instructional courses.

Author Bio:

Heather Revell is passionate about teaching music. She teaches students online and in person in her home studio in rural Northland, New Zealand. She is the Founder of *Music with Heather* and coaches beginner music teachers and teachers teaching beginner students. She is an author, a course creator, a coach, a mother of five and grandmother of eleven. She believes music makes intelligent children.

https://musicwithheather.com

HOW I BECAME A TEACHER OF TEACHERS

Bradley Sowash
United States

In 2006, I was asked by my publisher to attend a national music education conference to help market my new *That's Jazz* piano method. This was the first time I'd been around so many piano teachers, so I wasn't sure what to expect. Lacking sales experience, I asked any teacher who happened to pass by the exhibit booth, "Are you interested in teaching improvisation?" Most agreed to take a look if only out of politeness while admitting that teaching improvisation was unfamiliar, even a little scary. A few indignantly replied, "Why, certainly not." before proceeding down the aisle to peruse the latest editions of *Fur Elise*.

Have you noticed? Musicians tend to fall into two camps.

1. Eye players read written music: a skill that begins in traditional music lessons and becomes refined through experience. Reading musicians are able to play any style within their instrumental ability as long the music is fully notated. Eye players are

most at home performing well-rehearsed repertoire and may feel less comfortable improvising since that skill is often not included in their training.

2. Ear players learn by listening, imitating, and improvising. Often self-taught, these musicians enjoy the freedoms that come with creative music making. However, the size and stylistic range of their repertoire may be constrained by their musical experience and the limits of memorization.

Given the benefits and drawbacks of both approaches, it seems obvious that music students are best served by blending eye and ear skills. Unfortunately, this kind of comprehensive music education is still not the norm. One reason for the disconnect is that teachers understandably tend to teach as they were taught. It's not surprising, for example, that classically trained teachers are typically most comfortable with a written music curriculum. Of course, there's much to be said for traditional lessons that enable music reading, develops strong technique, and fosters appreciation for musical masterpieces. However, a curriculum that's focused solely on the page is inherently incomplete. Fortunately, more and more teachers are blending improvised popular styles with traditional repertory. Having ventured beyond their training, they want to know how to do it better. Teaching these teachers is a big part of why I crafted a course. Here's how it happened. Through book tours, conference presentations, articles, and more improvisation resources, I was becoming a music education influencer, but I wanted to do more to mentor forward-thinking teachers. So, when the Music Teachers National Association asked me to organize an unprecedented day long pop/jazz teacher training, my first call was to Leila Viss, an innovative classically trained piano teacher who I knew was interested in pop music and improvisation. Working together to line up presenters and navigate logistics, we weren't sure what to expect. So, when a standing-room-only crowd lined the walls to learn non-traditional ear playing skills from experts, we were delighted. Given the depth of interest, we decided to keep it going by launching *88 Creative Keys*, the first week-long workshop to focus solely on *off page* pedagogy. Meanwhile, as private lesson requests and speaking invitations were piling up, I began teaching live online group lessons and virtual teacher trainings just as video conferencing was becoming more widely available. Then and now, my focus is helping recovering classical pianists augment their reading skills by learning to improvise in themed courses such as *American Folk Songs, Bossa Nova, Intro to Blues, Jamming the Classics, Standards Step-by-Step*, etc. I feel privileged to enable a learning process that is sometimes life changing.

A student wrote:

"I had to share that this Sunday in church service I improvised on two Christmas songs after we finished singing and there was time to fill! I didn't even hesitate; I just knew where to go. It wasn't fancy but I can't believe it. You have taught me so much from the time my eyes were glued to every note. I have a million miles to go, but I'm oh so glad to see some progress. I'm loving every minute I play with no music in front of me. Thank you for freeing me from the chains of classical training."

Another participant shared this:

"I have been completely shaken out of my comfort zone and it has been an enormous amount of fun. I am not only looking at music differently, but also at the world in general because what is music if not a musician's universe? I have come to understand the value of a good ear and creativity, and this has changed how I teach my students."

It's as if they've discovered a hidden island where former read-only musicians choose their own notes, sometimes for the first time. After tasting the fruits of this creative paradise (that's actually been there all along), their enthusiasm for inviting others becomes contagious, saying things like "I want everyone to have the same freedom," and "I'll definitely be passing what I'm learning along to my students, so they get here sooner than I did!" Though I wouldn't have imagined it as a young jazz musician, it's immensely satisfying to preside over these kinds of transformations. Having previously seen myself as a performer who taught a bit on the side, I now regard myself as a teacher who occasionally performs. Along the way, it's led to lasting friendships with musicians who I might otherwise never have known. Since most of my "students" are piano teachers, it's nice to know that my courses and methods are being passed along. However, it's the interactive part of this online learning community that I enjoy most. Before, during, and after classes, participants share their progress, laugh, commiserate over shared challenges, support one another, gain confidence, and astonish themselves when they realize they really can make their own music.

Author Bio:

Bradley Sowash is a jazz pianist, composer, course creator, multi-instrumentalist, recording artist, author, and educator best known for his innovative live online group jazz piano classes, widely acclaimed keyboard improvisation books, and nine solo piano albums.

https://bradleysowash.com

WHY DID I DEVELOP AN ADULT INTENSIVE PIANO COURSE THAT INCLUDES HAPPY BIRTHDAY

Ivy Leung
Hong Kong

AFTER PASSING MY GRADE 8 PIANO EXAMINATION, I RUSHED TO my teacher and asked for a new song to play. Can you guess which masterpiece I asked for? A piece from Beethoven or Chopin? No. The answer was *Happy Birthday*. You may be curious as to why I asked for such a common and simple piece of music to play after passing the grade 8 piano examination. Let me tell you some of my background.

My teacher was a professional musician and a traditional teacher. She loved her students and took care of us. She always considered our examination results and gave many technical pieces for us to play. As her student, I really understood her expectations. I tried my best to practice every week and played good music for her in the lessons. She was a wonderful teacher. But deep in my heart, I really wanted to play some pieces other than classical music, demanding technical studies, and examination pieces. I liked the music that I heard on television and radio such as cartoon music and pop songs. I used my pocket money to buy some pop music books to play. However, I had mixed feelings about those books. The happy side was that I finally got some music of my favourite singers and cartoons. But on the opposite side, some of the scores were beyond my level, or had other issues such as wrong notes, errors in rhythms, and inadequate fingering arrangements. Therefore, although I got the music scores, I did not enjoy playing them. In those days, I always thought that I was not good enough to play pop music. As a result, I kept studying and aimed to learn *Happy Birthday* after passing the grade 8 piano examination.

After I graduated from university, I became a piano teacher for eight years. I found that many students were having the same thoughts as me. Although they did not refuse to play what I gave to them, they also desired to play pop music too. Some of the adult learners wanted to have piano lessons just for fun. However, they could not find teachers and materials which were suitable for them. Therefore, I began to collect some well-known music pieces such as nursery rhymes, cartoon music, film music, and pop songs. I classified them into different levels, such as beginners, moderate, and intermediate levels. Furthermore, I rearranged them again. The new arrangements included fingerings, effective harmonies, and recutting into suitable lengths for students. In addition, I designed some additional exercises for them to train their sense of rhythm and finger flexibilities. So that they were able to improve their performance skill while still enjoying playing the music. As a result, that was Why my *Intensive Pop Music Piano Course* was born!

As the learning time of the adult is very tight and limited, I designed a twenty-hour-course which they can finish within ten-months. After taking my ten-months course, they can play sixty pieces, including nursery rhymes, Chinese folk songs, Disney Cartoon music, and film music from the West, Japan, and Korea.

For the beginners level, the course was designed for new learners who have no music background and techniques. It includes the base knowledge of reading the music scores, hand positions, and body posture. They learn short pieces with single-line melodies and melodies with simple harmonies.

For the moderate level, after they have learned the base knowledge in the previous level, they can learn more difficult rhythmic patterns and a wider range of the keyboard. They can try some scales in different keys, such as keys up to two sharps and two flats keys. For the intermediate level, students will learn to harmonise the music with arpeggios in different patterns and use of pedals.

Many of my adult students told me that learning to play the piano was their childhood dream. Some of them found piano teachers to teach them how to play in the past but they did not enjoy the lessons until they were learning from me. They told me that they loved my materials. They did not believe that they could learn so many beautiful pieces in such a short period. Also, their learning spirit influenced their children, who were not willing to practice the piano.

As parents, they felt like they were their children's classmates and shared their learning experiences with good music that they both enjoyed learning and playing. The parent-child relationships were getting closer. Every time I see my adult students finish the whole intensive course I am impressed and encouraged to develop extensions to this course. I am so proud of their improvements. One important thing is they asked for further extension courses later. They had different needs such as they wanted to take part in the formal music examinations or they took their children to learn piano together or kindergarten teachers who needed to learn the pieces because of the working requirements.

The most inspiring thing is that they asked for my second set of intensive piano courses! It will be divided into different series, *Disney Princess series, 8os HK Pop Singers Series*, etc. For this course, there are many different future developments, and I am really excited to develop them one by one and hope more and more adults can play and enjoy the music they love to learn.

Learning music is not only a treasure for children, but learning music is also a treasure for adults.

Author Bio:

Ivy Leung CW, over 20 years teaching experience, course creator, chairperson of a HK registered charity music development association which holds music competitions and music oversea culture activities in Japan, Australia, and Taiwan.

www.hkget.com

FOLLOWING INTUITION

Lucinda Mackworth-Young
United Kingdom

WHAT ARE YOUR SIGNIFICANT MUSICAL MEMORIES? AND HOW have those events shaped your life? My first memory is aged four, running downstairs in our new house, and hearing my ten-year-old sister play the piano very fast. I don't remember hearing it before but I knew immediately that I wanted to play the piano very fast.

I was allowed to start lessons when I was eight. Not before, as my older sisters had started at that age, and, as my mother explained later, because she didn't want another child's practice to worry about. It was hard enough persuading the older two to do theirs. Lessons were fun and easy at first, but once I'd reached the stage where I needed to practice it was a different matter. The teacher was old-fashioned and formal. She didn't know how to encourage or teach specific steps for practicing, and she was probably, and understandably, tired with having to teach piano to children for a living.

However, at home I was playing (as you might have done too) *Chopsticks* and *Heart and Soul* over and over. Sometimes with a sister, sometimes by myself, making up variations. I didn't realise that I was improvising, and no one pointed out that *Chopsticks* consists of Chords I and V: I I I V in the first half ending with an imperfect cadence, then V V V I in the second half ending with a perfect cadence.

Neither did anyone explain that the chord progression of *Heart and Soul, The Way you Look Tonight* and a host of other 1950s songs, was I vi IV V. Enjoyable and potentially educational as it was, it was not considered proper practice.

Many years later, having still made no connections between such social and serious piano music, despite several theory exams, music "O" Level and distinctions in Grade 8 piano and clarinet, I was asked to play *Happy Birthday* at a party. I couldn't. I had no idea that only chords I, IV and V were needed. I just knew that I was unable to play anything without notation. Anything, that is, except the first section of a current Mozart sonata, and a Poulenc Novelette (hardly party music!).

Meanwhile some fifteen-year-old, who'd never had any piano lessons, was jamming out the latest pop tune. Which I couldn't do either. Was this an experience of yours? Rather humiliated, I wondered how any exam board could structure their standard piano exam syllabus so that even passionately committed, hard-working (I was by then), and highly successful piano pupils could be so crippled, unable to play without notation.

And throughout my life, which was filled with a deep love of music and dance, I had been having other realisations:

1. Lessons were made or marred by the quality of the teacher/pupil relationship or atmosphere in the room: My first teacher was good (later teachers assured me I'd had "a good grounding"), but lessons were not enjoyable to the extent that, at age ten, I'd wanted to give up. I wasn't allowed. But I was due to go to a new school, a ballet school because I wanted to be a ballet dancer, so I had a new teacher. The new teacher was nice.

I realised she thought I was good. Giving up never crossed my mind.

2. Pupils were not generally consulted about what they wanted to learn. They were just expected to get on with it, but that wasn't motivating. Although I liked my new teacher, I still didn't practice, except when exams were coming up. But would you have practised if, aged twelve, you were given a piece called *Little People of the Hills*? It was only when I was given what I immediately felt to be a proper piece of music, a Mozart sonata, that I was completely captivated. I couldn't believe the beauty of it and began to practise in earnest.

3. However good the teacher-pupil relationship and however much the music motivates, the teacher needs subject knowledge and expertise. Although the teacher at my ballet school gave me wonderful musical opportunities such as choir, madrigal group, a second instrument, music "O" level, taking part in music festivals, and singing with the boys' school's choral society, she wasn't a pianist. So, I didn't learn to articulate properly, use arm weight, or fully understand the pedals. And my forearms would stiffen up so swiftly that I wondered how anyone could possibly play a whole concerto. My third teacher with whom I took my Grade 8, was better, as was my college professor. But it wasn't until I'd graduated that I went to a teacher who taught me how to make a truly secure, comfortable, and professional sound.

4. Teachers need to use intuition and have a good psychological understanding of pupils - being able to pick up the subtle cues and clues from them and respond in a helpful way.

As a result, I:

a. became a music teacher who specialised in piano (sitting on a piano stool had become far more comfortable than dancing en pointe).

b. delved deeply into psychology to help musicians teach, learn, and perform more effectively and enjoyably without anxiety.

c. developed a step-by-step system so that classically trained piano players could learn to play by ear, improvise, and play spontaneously at social events.

d. gave workshops to teach musicians the steps of the dances they play, such as the minuet, mazurka, polonaise, etc.

e. performed as a pianist and chamber musician – my musical tastes having matured to embrace slow as well as fast music.

f. formed an association, *Music, Mind and Movement*, to build bridges between music, dance, and psychology, running courses and workshops.

Following many years of running a course to refresh and inspire Musicians, I was invited to direct and develop the *European Piano Teachers Association's Pedagogy Course* in 2007, with a team of like-minded colleagues. Now known as *The Piano Teachers' Course UK*, which offers face-to-face and online courses, including the original, innovative, and comprehensive Cert PTC, as well as courses leading to the DipABRSM and LRSM. Courses leading to Trinity's ATCL and LTCL are currently being developed. www.pianoteacherscourse.org.

My other courses, *Spontaneous Social Piano, Late Starter Piano* a series of Forums and How to play by ear and improvise are hosted by Benslow Music.

I also give workshops and webinars wherever invited such as *The Curious Piano Teachers, Piano Teaching Success, the Incorporated Society of Musicians,* and the *European Piano Teachers' Association.* And if any of my story has resonated with yours, you would be so welcome to join in!

Author Bio:

Pioneering International Director of the leading *Piano Teach-ers' Course UK*, Lucinda's publication, *Piano by Ear*, was finalist in the 2016 Music Teacher Awards, and *TUNING IN: Practical Psychology for Musicians* is also now an e-book.

https://www.lucinda-mackworth-young.co.uk/

WHO WILL RESCUE THE DAMSEL IN DISTRESS

Joanne Barker
Canada

HAVE YOU EVER FELT LIKE YOU WERE A CHARACTER IN A fairytale? Going from bowl to bowl trying to find the porridge that was not too hot or too cold, but 'just right'? Sitting on chair after chair and finding one was too hard, the next, too soft? Trying on that glass shoe only to find out it does not fit, no matter how hard you try? I have! For me that struggle was not about porridge, chairs, or shoes, but the quest to find a piano lesson course. Unlike a fairytale, there was no fairy Godmother, magic potion, or handsome prince to come to my rescue. However, just like in a fairytale, my struggle took me down some dark pathways and through some unexpected, challenging experiences along the way.

I started my career as an exuberant teenager, full of confidence, and excited to share my love for music. I wanted to give my students the most productive lessons that I could, so I did my research and started with the most current piano course available. My teaching career got off to a great start.

However, I soon felt frustrated with the flow of my lessons. As this feeling was developing, Prince Charming came into my life, and we were soon married. We moved 1300 miles north to an isolated community in the forest. There were no music book stores for hundreds of miles, so I continued using the course I had started with and made do by altering and revising pages to get a better fit. Living in the northern forest gave me an opportunity to spend time studying and reading. This helped me to form an even clearer understanding of what I wanted for my students. After only one year living in the north, we decided to return home.

Living near a large city provided many opportunities to attend workshops to further my professional development. I bought numerous piano course method books to explore, most of which ended up on my bookshelf, unused. I began offering group lessons, but after a few years, the nagging feeling of frustration crept back into my life. I still had not found the piano course that fit. Just like in those fairytales, life threw some challenges in my direction. Within a four-year period, I had three major knee surgeries, and was diagnosed with breast cancer. This was a very intense and difficult period of my life. It was like being lost in that dark, scary fairytale forest at times. I had barely recovered from the knee surgeries when I underwent cancer surgery, followed by chemotherapy and radiation. Weeks before my cancer diagnosis, I became an *Ultimate Music Theory Certified Teacher* and soon after, began creating games for *Ultimate Music Theory*. It was a relief to know that I had a solid theory course to use. Thanks to *UMT*, I was now a confident music theory teacher. This only fueled my frustration that I did not have the piano course that fit as well. That same year, I decided to switch to a new piano course. I had such high hopes that this course would be the right fit. However, it felt all wrong. It lacked flow of concepts and had very little review built in. I had to do something. Part way through the year, I scrapped it and went back to a course I had used years previously.

Thankfully, I was able to keep teaching during cancer treatment, only missing a few days each round of chemo, and a few weeks when I was sick with viral pneumonia. After my cancer treatment ended, medical follow-up appointments and tests seemed never-ending. I had a breast cancer recurrence scare. Thankfully, it was a false alarm. I was diagnosed with chemotherapy induced peripheral neuropathy (nerve damage) in my hands and feet.

Chemotherapy sped up arthritic degeneration in my body, including my lower back, which meant more physiotherapy appointments. Surgeons recommended three surgeries: finger joint replacement, thumb joint fusion and knee replacement. I wanted nothing to do with more surgery, so I decided to take control of what I could at a time when it seemed I had little control. I modified my lifestyle and vowed to continue with physiotherapy to manage pain and put off the surgeries. Despite all my medical challenges, my studio was thriving. I had created a hybrid lesson system of group and private lessons which was working well for my students, but still there was the issue of finding the right piano course to use. I was feeling frustrated and defeated. What was I to do? Was I stuck using material that didn't work for me? Unlike the fairytale character, I may not have been tasting bowl after bowl of porridge, but I was going from course to course, desperately seeking the right one. Like the glass shoe in the fairytale, the courses I had been using just didn't fit my teaching style! My frustration grew and grew. There had to be a solution. One day it occurred to me: I could create my own piano course! The damsel in distress can save herself, can't she? I definitely had the fortitude to overcome obstacles. I had learned to walk after repeated knee surgeries, and how to thrive after cancer treatment. I had experienced intense pain, physically and emotionally, yet I could still find joy in my life.

While I could not control what life threw at me, I could

choose to take control over how I dealt with it. My quest changed from finding to crafting my own piano course. I used guides and syllabi as I methodically laid out concepts and started work composing the music I needed. After months of hard work, I had six levels ready to debut. Just like modern fairytale heroines, I didn't need a hero to rescue me. I had the power to save myself. All I had to do was take the determination I gained from my life experiences and use it to craft my own piano course.

My quest, my Why, was driven by frustration and fuelled by my determination to find the perfect piano course. I knew it existed; I just needed to find it. The resolution to my quest was not where I expected it to be. It wasn't in a bookstore, it was within reach all long, I just had to craft it myself. I hope your Why will empower you to undertake a challenge. The satisfaction is more than worth the effort.

Author Bio:

Joanne Barker, *UMTC* Elite Educator, Piano Teacher, Composer, *UMT* Creative Designer, International Best-Selling Author. Joanne has successfully crafted the hybrid piano course used by her students in her piano studio.

https://UltimateMusicTheory.com/

THE POWER OF A POSITIVE MENTAL ATTITUDE

David A. Jones
United Kingdom

HOW I WENT FROM THE VERGE OF GIVING UP MUSIC completely to successfully pitching a multi-million-dollar musical idea to one of the world's most respected Animation Studios.

England - 1990.

The Main Theatre was filled with my fellow college students, our families, and friends. I hadn't understood my music despite asking the teacher for help some weeks previously. The teacher dismissed me, as I should understand this and just do the work. I was nervous and poorly prepared, so I hardly played during the performance. Petrified, my hands just hovered over the keyboard; I prayed for the piece to end so I could get off stage.

As there were around twenty in the band, the audience couldn't identify my non-performance. After an eternity, the piece finished. Cheers and applause erupted from the crowd. I'd gotten away with it.

Then my music teacher stood up, introduced each performer

one by one. When the teacher got to me, they pointed at me and announced:

"Miming on keyboard is David Jones."

The theatre went deathly silent.

All eyes were on me. I think the audience died a bit for me. I'd been publicly humiliated - called out by my teacher.

My music was simple Figured Bass - easy to learn if you understand chords, which I did. However, I'd not been shown that link to chords. Students should not need to decode what is being taught, yet decoding is what I found myself doing. Little did I know that the extra steps I was having to do were training me toward a successful musical future, despite a certain teacher, not because of.

At school, I was quiet, lonely, and lacked confidence. I had previously felt like a second-rate student, almost a joke. This took me so much lower. Maybe my teacher thought *surely everyone understands this easy bit?* No. Not everyone learns in the same way. A single key will not fit all locks.

I can't dance, I'm not a great singer, and my wonderful wife and children think my cooking is interesting. There are many things I'm awful at. I'm happy to state my shortcomings because hopefully it adds a little humility and credence to the next sentence: I was totally confident and competent in my chord knowledge and improvising around chord structures.

Although I'd been classically taught from the age of eight, I would often jam with my inspirational parents, friends, and family in bands. So being given a chord sheet or notation and improvising over it was something I'd done for many years. However, as I was doing something different to the norm of class work, my college teacher made me feel like I was somehow cheating - like I was performing third-rate mock music.

Figured Bass should have played to my strengths. I should have excelled in this performance. Instead, it resulted in a huge mental downturn in my confidence and progress. I almost left college, giving up music for good. I like to think that the public ridicule by my teacher was a moment of horrendously bad judgement. It is ironic, but that teacher had been one of my favourites too.

From age ten I'd spend hours composing, arranging, recording, and mixing. I wanted to write music for games, films, and cartoons. I would fast-track the notation in piano pieces, seeing shapes and patterns of harmony and learning by ear instead of solely relying on sheet music. What I grew to feel were immense weaknesses were actually my strengths, which, if they'd been spotted and nurtured, would have helped me progress faster.

Over the years, I did have some excellent music teachers: Barbara Miller at School, Andy Hickey at University, and most of all, my teacher for many years, the awesome Ray Kelly. He taught the way I learnt, like all great educators should. Ray had faith in me, helped my confidence grow, and suggested I join him at the local music store to teach little ones. I loved their endless sense of fun and their joy when we played as a band. I'd found an audience who liked me, maybe because I had the same crazy sense of humour as them.

Early in my teaching career, I remember a particular lesson. I was horrified at a lost expression on one of my student's faces: a look that I must have had, years before.

And that was it.

I was immediately on a mission.

I committed to researching and developing pedagogy to demystify music for my students who found any aspect of our lessons tricky. I did everything I could to communicate in an inspirational, intuitive way. Above all, I would teach how they learnt. I mixed in my love of writing and recording by creating crazy songs to help students learn whilst having fun.

I shared common goals with friends and family and *Presto Music School* was formed. Mountains can be moved with a can-do attitude, so we created the *#PositivelyPresto* movement for our students who have flourished. They are better than we were at the same point in our studies.

I was approached by Casio and the London College of Music who asked if we could turn our class work into courses. Using the *#PositivelyPresto* mindset ourselves, we said yes, and we were promptly commissioned to write our *Piano, Keyboard and Theory Course*, plus exam pieces. I networked further, gaining amazing commercial music production jobs which lead to scoring for films. We dodged an aggressive take-over by a 3rd party because after everything I'd gone through, no one was taking anything from my family and my children's potential legacy. In that moment, I learnt what was driving me, and I was growing some serious confidence!

Putting our educational and composing work together, we took an idea to the Cannes TV / Film marketing festival. We connected with the creative genius of *Sparky Animation Studios' KC Wong and Team*. We became co-creators on the project that became *Rhythm Warriors* - our new TV series currently in production - my dream job. If I can do it, anyone can.

So why do I feel we are well-placed to write courses and teach? It's because of our unique background of *Failing Student* to *Formidable Success*: Our discoveries, how we discovered them, and how we applied it all to get amazing results for our students. I want to make a positive difference in the world, offering solutions to others on subjects I'd painfully struggled with. Above all, I do it for the thing that drives me most: my family.

Author Bio:

David A Jones (BAPMR): Director of *Presto Music School*, course creator, Award-Winning Film Composer, Co-Creator of the Musical TV Series *Rhythm Warriors* produced by *Emofront and Presto Music Production* in association with *Sparky Animation Studios*.

www.PrestoMusicSchool.co.uk

TRANSFORMED FROM ORDINARY TO CONFIDENT SINGERS

Benny Ng
Australia

IMAGINE YOU ARE IN A DARK ROOM. YOU HAVE BEEN TOLD there is a piano in the room but you cannot see it. You fumble around the room and finally find it. Sitting on the piano stool, you try to play the piano. There is just not enough light in the room for you to even see the keys. So, you feel your way around the keys and manage to play "Heart and Soul" with plenty of wrong notes. You stand up now. Taking three steps back and away from the piano, you try to play Heart and Soul. You feel confused and silly. Now, come back to me.

Why did I take you through that? It is because that is the challenge most singers go through when they are learning to sing. When you play a guitar or a piano, you can see and touch the instrument. When you want to play a note, you just pluck the string or hit the key. There is no guesswork. Your voice or vocal apparatus/mechanism is inside of your body. How are you supposed to play something you cannot see or touch?

That was the challenge I faced when I first started learning to sing. You see, singing did not come easily to me. I am a high male voice or tenor. I could sing quite high but my throat would tense up so much that a squealing sound would come out instead. I would then yell to make my voice sound fuller when I sang high notes. I would sing out of tune due to the lack of breath support and sufficient awareness of the melody. My lower register notes were less than stellar because I did not work on them very much. I started taking singing lessons when I was seventeen.

However, it was not until when I was in university eight years later that I started to unlock the secrets of singing. As a detail-oriented person, I was not given the information I needed to fully understand how the voice worked. Many of the private lessons I had were not structured for getting the best results in singing. I struggled for a long time and developed many bad habits I had to unlearn for years.

Determined to gain control of my voice and sing with confidence, I enrolled in the world-renowned Sydney Conservatorium of Music. It was there that the art of singing gradually revealed its secrets to me. I spent countless hours in the library, borrowed and studied every book on vocal technique I could find. I would pore over research papers from voice science journals. I read textbooks from cover to cover. It eventually dawned on me that there was an all-encompassing concept that was the foundation of singing. This concept underlies almost all vocal techniques - no matter the style or genre.

It is called the Open Throat Concept.

When I started applying this concept to my singing, my progress skyrocketed. It was as if everything I had learned about singing fell into place. Things I could not do before now felt easy to do. I was on cloud nine.

Shortly after graduating, I began my career as a singing teacher/vocal coach. As an avid planner in my everyday life, I naturally planned each and every private lesson I taught. The

Open Throat Concept would form the cornerstone of my lesson plans. It was so gratifying to see my students go from 'can't carry a tune in a bucket' to singing in front of an audience.

After ten years of private vocal coaching, a syllabus was inadvertently created. I wanted this knowledge to benefit as many aspiring singers as possible - amateur or professional.

One question I always get is: "Can anyone learn to sing or is it a talent you have to be born with?"

The voice is definitely an instrument you can learn to 'play'. However, it is also one of the hardest instrument to master because you cannot see or touch your voice. You have to visualize it. You have to increase your awareness of bodily sensations like never before. You need to develop neural networks for these new, fine motor skills. Most of all, you need to make all parts of your 'instrument' work as a whole. As human beings, we are emotional creatures. Like it or not, our feelings are prone to get hurt by what people say about our voice. It is not uncommon for someone to stop singing for the rest of their lives because their choir teacher in primary school told them they could not sing.

What a tragedy!

Your voice is your identity. Your mental health and happiness are inextricably linked to your voice.

Driven by the desire to help as many people as I could to be proud of their voice, without me having to be in the same room or even the same time zone, I created *Singing Confidence Academy*. It is an online singing academy that helps closet singers become confident singers.

Based on the syllabus of my private vocal coaching, my goal for *Singing Confidence Academy* is to help people around the world gain control of their voice, sing with confidence and be proud of their singing voice. I made over $1000 in sales, one month after launching the academy.

It is an amazing feeling when I get emails from people around the world, thanking me for helping them sing better. I always say: if your voice is healthy, and you can speak without pain or your voice sounding too hoarse, then you can learn to 'play' it well. Imagine what a happier place this world would be when more people realize they could learn to sing well if they would just learn how to do it.

My mission is to help people realize it is not *if* they can sing well but *what* they need to do to get there.

And I am just getting started.

Author Bio:

Benny Ng is a vocalist, songwriter, course creator, and singing teacher. His courses help singers gain control of their voice, sing with confidence, and be proud of their singing voice. Learn more and get your free *Singing Confidence Training Package* at *Top Singing Secrets*.

https://www.topsingingsecrets.com

IT'S ALL ABOUT MY STUDENTS

Caroline Joy Quinn
United States

YEARS AGO, I HAD A DEVASTATING CONVERSATION WITH A college professor that left me completely shattered. Looking down at me, my professor told me that when he looked at me, he saw lights on, and no one home. At that time, I was recovering from a difficult past, very insecure, and struggling to find my way. His comment made me want to fall into the floor and disappear forever. To be fair to my professor, I didn't present as a winner. Let's hear it for late bloomers. That said, I vowed that no student of mine would ever leave my home without knowing that I was his or her biggest fan. Although my students may never play at Carnegie Hall, they will always know that I believed in them. My course, *Joyful Sounds*, is designed to meet individuals right where they are musically and personally.

Understanding that everyone is not the same and assessing each student's ability is a huge part of my program. I am the students' musical cheerleader, and my course is about celebrating strengths, not criticizing weaknesses. Every student has his or her own story. I can best serve my students by listening, learning, and implementing what is meaningful to them. Without meaning there is no connection. And without connection, there can be no joy.

Joyful Sounds has evolved over the years. At first, I relied heavily on lesson books. Later, while teaching at a boarding school in England, I prepared students for the National Music Exams, a graded course of classical repertoire and technique with no room for improvisation or composing. After moving to Seattle, my course material was a combination of lesson books and supplemental sheet music with many participating in recitals and festivals. Improvisation and composing were also introduced. However, over time, my teenagers seemed to lose interest in their lesson books, requesting to play their favourites instead. They wanted to play *Bohemian Rhapsody* instead of Bach. It was time to shake things up.

Branching out and teaching new styles was the next necessary step. Delighted, and now highly motivated playing their favourites, my students began to exceed all my expectations. Connecting with their music was incredibly empowering as they developed their own musical passions.

Designing lessons based on individual abilities and personalities is part of my mission statement. Lesson books for beginners are useful tools, but even beginners have their favourites. Like my older students, they also create a binder with their top tunes. And yes, it takes extra time to tailor-make lessons. Is it worth the effort? Absolutely. What else is part of my course? Understanding theory is fundamental, creating a foundation for improvisation and composition. There is a freedom to interpret the music in a way that is meaningful to each individual. Seeing and hearing the rise and fall of the music, students discover the art of expressive playing, experiencing deep connections as their musical story unfolds.

In my program, there is space to address musical preferences and personal needs. In my opinion, both are equally important. Relationships are key. Growing together as musicians and human beings, sharing our joys and sorrows, we make our world better through music. No one cares about what you know, until they know how much you care. This truth came home to me in a recent conversation that I had with my son. As a leader in the military, instead of assigning physical training and leaving his soldiers on their own, he runs with them, building trust over time. The same is true in teaching. Over time, trusting relationships are formed. Music touches everyone in different ways, and I am passionate about teaching whatever my students wish to learn. One lesson, one scale, one line at a time, we, as teachers, can inspire our students, helping to shape their lives for the good.

Although I could write a book of all the lives that have been part of my story, here are just a few snapshots.

One young girl struggled with a debilitating fear of failure. Music that she perceived to be too hard caused great stress and frustration. A new plan was needed, and I started writing my own arrangements for her favourite tunes. She was tickled pink with my arrangement of *Shake It Off* by Taylor Swift written with her strengths in mind. Diving in with new-found interest and enthusiasm, my once shy little girl, now played her special song with pride. She went on to learn more challenging pieces and even signed up for her school talent show. Our lessons gave her time and space to address her personal needs, instilling a new level of confidence in her playing and beyond.

Another student, a brilliant, but very intense young man arrived for his lesson appearing anxious and stressed and needed to escape outside pressures. After a little chat, we began to work on his piece, and I was completely blown away watching him pour himself into every chord. His interpretation and creative touches were unexpected and amazing, breathing hope into his soul, empowering, and inspiring him to carry on.

The glorious *Moonlight Sonata* is generally reserved for an older student, so when my ambitious middle school student insisted on learning it, I was concerned. Very concerned. But seeing her determination, I decided to trust her judgement. Working line by line, page by page, noticing all the accidentals throughout, she soldiered on. To be honest, it wasn't a picnic. Although she adored the music, she was not thrilled about following all the fingering and rhythms. Thankfully, with much prompting, she did the hard work needed in preparation for our year end recital. The magic of music drew her into its circle of beauty by creating a successful story.

Another student is an extremely busy partner in her law firm and carving out time to practice is challenging. There is always grace. I love teaching her, and we have fun together. As a beginner she learned quickly, and through the years she mastered one piece at a time and is now playing advanced pieces. I am super proud of her accomplishments. When asked why she loves piano, she shared that her lessons are an escape that feeds her soul. I agree.

Joyful Sounds continues to enrich many lives by providing music that speaks to their hearts. When our students find satisfaction and joy in their music, we, as teachers, also experience satisfaction and joy. Who could ask for anything more?

Author Bio:

Caroline Joy Quinn, ARCT, Bach. Sacred Music, Accredited Music Therapist, Children's Author, Teacher, Course Creator, *UMTC* Elite Educator, Arranger and Publisher.

https://www.facebook.com/caroline.j.quinn.7

WHY IMPROVISE

Thulane Akinjide-Obonyo
Zimbabwe

FEAR GRIPPED ME AS THOUGH I WAS ABOUT TO DIE. AT THIS rate, I would never make it. I felt exhausted, and I really could not think what to do. It was as though a sort of madness had gripped my mind and entered my entire body. I really did not know what to do. What had happened?

I had been asked to play my first improvised solo. I was in front of a crowd of twenty people in a workshop at the Harare International's Festival of the Arts.

I had just started learning the saxophone four months ago and here was a saxophone guru, Andy Sheppard, asking me to improvise; I froze up, and I could not perform. Luckily my teacher stepped in to stop the humiliation. From that day forward, I could not get to grips with improvisation. I studied a lot about it, and I learned to play the D blues scale to compensate. I was a great reader but when it came to improvising, I could not hear myself think, I simply went with whatever scale I thought worked best.

Forget the idea of trying to express myself, this was out of the question; I was just trying to survive the ordeal. How could I get through improvising as soon as possible and get back to the safety of reading sheet music?

You can imagine my relief when I learned that there was a genre of music where you did not have to improvise. My sadness turned to joy when I found classical saxophone playing. All you had to do was read from the sheet music, and I knew that I could do that.

The crushing shame that I felt disappeared; I immersed myself in classical saxophone studies. It made sense to me as my father is a classical music superfan. I would listen to his record collection and reproduce what I heard. This was the ultimate way to learn to play saxophone. And learn to play I did. Shame left me, and I would practice for three hours every day in high school. I would find innovative ways around the most difficult passages.

I would practice first thing in the morning from 5.45am to 6:15am, then I would practice in the afternoon from 1pm to 2pm and then I would make sure to practice again in the evening from 7pm to 8:30pm which was my big practice.

Over time my hard work really paid off; I was able to progress through the graded exams and reach the coveted Grade 8 ABRSM saxophone status when I was 21. For a kid from Zimbabwe, I had arrived or so I thought, but worse tragedies were to come. I did not know that my most challenging days were just around the corner.

"Voice, voice those chords," I remember Janice shouting. It did not help that she was a bodacious blonde whom I had fallen in love with and who was an accomplished jazz singer and jazz pianist. We were prepping for my audition for the Royal Academy of Music which was just down the road from my grandmother's flat. Misunderstandings were common in those days. I really could not understand jazz at all, and I had been told that I did not stand a chance of passing the audition. To make things worse, Janice was accepted when she was seventeen and given early admission. Intelligence counts for nothing in the world of music. I simply could not hack it. I was told not to attend the audition as I would embarrass myself.

I did attend the audition, and I was terrible. They spared telling me that I did not get in and instead sent a letter to Grandma's place. Really this was the most painful period of my life. I had been playing the saxophone for nine years, and I was refused entry to one of the most prestigious music conservatories in the world, and I lost my chance to be with a beautiful angel. Feeling crushed was an understatement.

Ten years later, I had figured out why I had crashed and burned. I realised how to improvise, and, in the end, it was not what the RCM would teach me. I felt empowered the day I realised what improvisation really was and how it was built on easy to learn and easy to understand principles.

I was inspired by a wonderful saxophonist, a busker who would play at the corner of Selfridges. Inspiration struck me when I heard the power of his lament when he played *Careless Whisper* with a tone so powerful it cut your soul. I bought him dinner one day and asked for his secrets and he told me. They were really simple and astonishing.

I realise just how crushing the inability to express yourself on your chosen instrument could be to many, many people. I am a saxophonist, and even though I did not go to the RCM, I understand your pain more deeply than most others will because I did fail, and it took me ten years to learn how to improvise effectively.

Nowadays, I have a lot on my plate, and this is why I made a course to teach people how to improvise. If you were to ask my Why? Well, my Why is to ask, "Why does the bluebird sing? Why do children cry? Why does man suffer?"

I cannot answer these questions and quite seriously the questions are not important. What is, is that you express yourself. Not only do millions of people go to the grave without expressing themselves but millions die each year because they do not have a creative outlet for their emotions, whether it be pain, grief, love, joy, or whimsy.

Technology can be used to empower or destroy. Creating a course allows you to use it to empower and heal the world, as with the internet, it can reach those who need it most.

Author Bio:

Thulane Akinjide-Obonyo, is a professional saxophonist, course creator, and saxophone coach. He specialises in teaching people how to play the saxophone by ear so that they may express themselves through the music that lies deep in their hearts.

https://www.facebook.com/playsaxnow

A COURSE - OF COURSE

Frances Balodis
Canada

WHEN I WROTE *MUSIC FOR YOUNG CHILDREN* IN MARCH 1980, I wanted to create good solid learning with fun. I became a Registered Music Teacher in 1976 and knew several other music teachers who were excellent music teachers and who were very serious about their music teaching. I wanted to be serious and have fun along with my students and their parents.

That was different from most music teachers who taught their students without a parent being present. I wanted a triangle of fun and learning.

The Music for Young Children plan was to have up to six children and their parents in a group. Group learning in 1980 was not popular. Also, music instruction for three-year-olds was not popular. *MYC* had a BIG mountain to climb.

Soon people started inquiring about teaching *MYC*. So, I set up teacher training sessions. Why would a music teacher need to take a teacher training session to teach *MYC*? *MYC* had a playful approach and a multi-faceted learning-style approach. There is singing, movement, composition, keyboard, listening, history, harmonization, and theory – and most piano teachers are mainly teaching the instrument.

At the teacher training session, the teachers learned about solfege – and the value of arm and hand signs. The teachers learned how to teach composition. Many teachers did not consider themselves composers, so this was a real stretch for them. They learned the value of singing – teaching concepts through song and the value of pitch matching. The history of the composers was taught in a tiny vignette way – something that would interest the young student. Listening was valuable – listening for dynamics, tempo, and pitch. Things that a music teacher might take for granted with an older child need to have more focus for the younger one.

The value and fun of harmonization is a big switch for traditional piano teachers. What are the three most important chords in every key? Every *MYC* child knows they are I, IV, V. Many traditional piano teachers are amazed how exciting this is. When they learn to harmonize, the world of music freedom opens up.

The training that I had through my MEd. (from Acadia University) in working with children who have learning challenges and difficulties and from DISC and Neuro-Linguistic Programming, I learned the valuable skills for facilitating learning for all ages – especially young children in music education. I shared this knowledge of preferential learning styles with teachers in the teacher training course for *MYC*. This really set *MYC* teachers on a path to success with this course.

When all these things were learned, the teacher then needed to learn how to put it all together – into a one hour, interesting, and fun package. The main point here is 'up, down, up, down'. If the child and parent sit too long, they can become distracted or bored, and if they stand too long, they can become wiggly So, the main idea is to have a 'down' activity followed by an 'up' activity. The sixty-minute class then goes quickly. When a student says, "Oh, is it time to go already?" you know the hour has been fun and successful.

Routine is important. Every class begins the same way – with an opening song. Every class ends the same way – with a closing song. Every class has the same activities – singing, keyboard composing, rhythm ensemble, listening, game playing, ensemble playing at the keyboard, and for the older children solo playing. The children and parents look forward to the routine and become accustomed to it.

Parents began to realize they were learning right along with their children. They found out that they too must keep up as the children were enjoying it and quickly soaking up the concepts. The parent was encouraged to help their child practice at home. It was usually just the children that practiced, but the parents often discovered that they too needed to practice. And speaking of practicing, there was a homework sheet that the child could check off - what is to be practiced and how to practice. it This is a good goal setting sheet.

The concept of a 'course' took off. Children and parents loved it, and teachers enjoyed it. Then, parents asked if they could have a a course of their own. So, they too have a course called *Music Your Best Choice.* This course has the same principles as the children's course with a more mature repertoire. This course is taught individually or in groups.

The idea of a course is now history as *MYC* is taught in many countries around the world. Our daughter, Olivia Riddell who is the International Director teaches many teacher-training sessions virtually. She and *MYC* Coordinators monitor how *MYC* teachers present the program – sometimes this is done in person, sometimes virtually. It is important to maintain quality – and *MYC* has done a great job of consistency and quality for 41 years. Students can transfer from one teacher to another, from one country to another and seamlessly slip from one *MYC* teacher to another, from one *MYC* class to another. This is a real kudo, not always found in other courses.

Some *MYC* teachers have been teaching *MYC* for decades. They really enjoy the support they receive through *MYC* head office and through their coordinator. They view their *MYC* teaching as their job and career, and they are proud to have recitals and other events of quality.

It was important to have a course that would conclude with Conservatory Grade One Piano. This gives *MYC* a standard that others understand. When *MYC* students graduate, their next teacher knows what these students know. Also, many students write their theory exams from the Conservatory. This is important as it gives a strong foundation for the students – and one that other teachers understand. The Conservatory can be one in Canada, England, or any Conservatory around the world. One that is understood by parents and teachers in their own culture.

Having a course that is 41 years old gives credibility to *Music for Young Children*. I am proud that it has developed and is maintained as a course of high standard. Students who are graduates of *MYC* are now teaching *MYC* and bringing their own children to this course they love so dearly.

MYC makes learning fun for me is truly the theme song of this course.

Author Bio:

Frances Mae Balodis MEd., ARCT, LCCN(H), LCNCM(H), RMT, MYCC is founder (in 1980) of *Music for Young Child*ren® and cofounder of *CLU*™ certified NLP and an Accredited DISC Training provider and *MYC* Course Creator. Frances is Director of The Muskoka Men of Song.

https://www.myc.com

A COURSE CREATION JOURNEY AROUND THE WORLD

Sarah Lyngra
United States

When I was living in Copenhagen, Denmark, just after I got married in 1997, I was one of the few English-speaking piano teachers around. I ordered most of my music by a long-distance telephone call. (The telephone was attached to the wall, and calls were really expensive.) Sheet music took a long time to arrive and needed to be ordered from the United States months in advance. I crafted a course because teaching materials were not available in the country in which I was teaching.

In Denmark, there weren't too many teachers who taught young children. Many parents who wanted piano lessons for their young children didn't play an instrument themselves. I created a course which was easy enough for both the children and their parents to follow along with at home.

In addition to teaching young students, I also taught students who had learning disabilities and visual impairments. That's when I started using color to make it easier for students who struggle with learning how to read. Color enhanced music wasn't commonly used at the time. I created courses because there were very few materials for students who have learning disabilities.

When we moved to the Middle East after our son was born, the issues of not having sheet music available were compounded. At the time, there was a risk of sheet music being confiscated when it was shipped to the country in which we lived. The internet was still in its infancy, and digital downloads of anything didn't exist. Our internet was a spotty dial-up connection. While I returned to the United States once a year and would buy music for my students at that time, it was expensive and wasn't always a fit for what I needed. I continued to create my own courses because it was all I had available at the time.

Course creation up to this point was on paper. I used the computer as a word processor to create worksheets and engrave music. In 2013, Karen X. Cheng created a website (now defunct) called *Give It 100*. The premise was that over 100 days people would upload one ten-second video every day to move themselves toward a goal. I used the site for various projects, one of them was a mini course on learning to play the piano. Over the course of two years, I created over six hundred ten-second videos. I created a mini course on learning the keys of the piano to learn how to create short videos.

The author Daniel Coyle wrote *The Talent Code* in 2009. At the same time, he had a blog, which is where I learned of Karen X. Cheng's video challenge. It featured Salman Khan who started the Kahn Academy in 2008. Khan was a pioneer of the flipped classroom where students watch videos at home and use class time to go deeper into the subject matter. His videos were and are short, basic, and each cover a single topic. This was fascinating to me. Khan started the Khan Academy because the parents of autistic kids would write to him thanking him for making the videos. It helped their kids learn things that they couldn't learn easily in a normal classroom. Around this time, our son was diagnosed with a learning disability which had a visual component. I create courses to help students who don't learn the way playing piano is traditionally taught.

Because of the visual component of my son's learning disability, we were in and out of the developmental optometrist's office for over twelve years. I sat in countless hours of vision therapy and did a lot of the exercises at home with Nikolai. I developed relationships with the optometrists and therapists and learned a great deal about how visual systems work.

Creating courses and course materials helped me refine how I was teaching and condense it to techniques which have been effective in teaching both students who have learning difficulties or those who don't.

Digital technology has now exploded. It is so much easier to create videos, graphics, worksheets, and because of the music xml file format, creating color enhanced music takes minutes instead of the months it took even five years ago. While technology helps normal people, it helps those with disabilities in many more ways. Think about how helpful subtitles are. They are crucial to those with hearing impairments, but also make life nicer for those of us who aren't there yet. These days, I am creating courses with videos and digital files to make music more accessible for all students, not just those with impairments.

During the early days of the pandemic in 2020, I was in France doing a teach-online-piano-lessons experiment. I was shut in a 500-square-foot apartment by myself for three months, 23 hours of the day. Fortunately, since I was already teaching online, I had a computer, a piano, and time. This was an opportunity to experiment with making short courses on learning specific pieces. I created an online course which teaches the Adagio movement of the *Moonlight Sonata* one measure at a time with one video for each measure.

Since returning to the United States in mid 2020, I create and craft courses on things I need for my students that I can't find anywhere else. I create courses because by doing so, I continue to learn new ways of doing old things. I can refine and improve how I teach. And, because a lot of what I do focuses on teaching students with learning difficulties, I can share what I have done with other teachers, so they have another tool to use with their students.

Author Bio:

Sarah Lyngra, owner of *Yellow Cat Publishing*, LLC, and online course creator at *Teach Piano Online* and *Couch to Concert Hall* has been teaching students around the world to play the piano for over 25 years.

www.teachpianoonline.com

IT'S NOT WHAT, IT'S HOW

Paul Myatt
Australia

IT WAS THE CUP OF KNOCKED OVER ORANGE JUICE THAT REALLY frustrated Mum. It happened at least once a month. I'd be sitting listening to the radio and playing the breakfast table piano. Of course, there was no piano, I was just dreaming that there was. The occasional flourish at the end of a phrase would send the hand-squeezed cup of juice all over the floor.

The juice incident was just one of the catalysts for Mum deciding I needed music lessons. I look back and feel so thankful for Mum giving me the opportunities to learn in the ways that I did. My somewhat unconventional music education experiences gave me so much insight into how teaching instrumental music needed to change. It led to my passion for creating teaching courses for those who are keen to escape the shackles of the 19th-century methods that continue to purvey our profession.

Honestly, I don't remember how many tablecloths were destroyed by juice stains before my parents decided they would buy me a piano. Only they didn't. It was back in the groovy 1970s and the electronic organ had become the star instrument of the day. That and one of my dad's staff members wanted to offload her instrument so she could purchase the latest model. Nothing's changed really, in the 1970's it was electronic organs, today, it's iPhones! Everyone wants the new model.

When this beast of an instrument arrived, I was so excited. My eyes were agog. There were many buttons, sounds, and rhythms that I spent months just exploring.

We lived in the country and moved around a lot as my dad climbed the corporate ladder in the banking profession. There weren't many music teachers around and so, at nine years of age when this beautiful box of exciting sounds and buttons came into my life, I had received little music training.

The organ came with 6 audio cassettes and 200 pieces of music. Not knowing that I was supposed to read the music first, I started listening to the cassettes and began teaching myself by working out what the music meant. This was the equivalent of what my students do with YouTube today. So, essentially, I taught myself.

And teach myself I did for at least six months until finally, Mum signed me up for lessons. These were fun and I experienced a wide range of music from classical to contemporary. I loved playing along with the rhythms as they kept me in time. I also learned all the chords I needed to be able to play a lot of songs. I started playing at the church around the age of thirteen and was soon on duty every Sunday morning till the end of high school.

Fear not dear reader, probably just like you, I also had a very traditional experience steeped in 19th-century instrumental teaching pedagogy, learning only through reading. At school, I had French horn lessons. I was away the day they were giving out the cool instruments like saxophone or trumpet and ended up with the horn.

At my third lesson, I had decided that the 8 bars of Bach that

I had practiced the previous week would sound infinitely better with a bit of swing and improvisation. Naively, I announced to my teacher the reasons why my version was infinitely better than the original, only to be swiftly informed that such ventures into improvisation and creativity were not appropriate for ten-year-old boys who know nothing.

I have shared a music education journey with thousands of kids over the past thirty years. At the start of my career, I retreated to those 19th-century teaching practices and quickly realised that if I was to be a successful teacher, I needed to resort to different techniques. I didn't realise it then, that this was the start of *Whole Body Learning* and why I started writing courses for piano teachers.

The first courses were for piano teachers working at *Forte School of Music*. Business partner, colleague and best friend, Gillian Erskine and I created *Forte School of Music* in 1993. To grow Forte, we needed to empower teachers to find confidence in this new and innovative way to teach kids called *Whole Body Learning*. Now with nearly 8,000 students in the network, we continue to develop and enhance our teaching courses.

Over 100 years ago, Orff, Dalcroze, and Kodály were trying to change the way music education was taught. To move away from the 19th-century traditions of reading the music and then playing, towards exploration, singing, moving, playing, and finally reading. When I look back to my childhood, I realise that this was how I was taught organ. It was that initial learning experience that gave me the musical foundations to be a successful French horn player and later transfer all those skills to the piano.

When teachers are able to give students a broader musical foundation, students will stay interested and learn for longer and are more likely to go on to develop a life-long pleasure of playing music. This can only happen through empowering teachers to explore new ways of teaching. *Whole Body Learning* courses show teachers how to embrace the natural learning process (listening, singing, playing, reading, and writing), the importance of moving to learn, and including the use of technology.

A tradition of the UK and all British colonies around the world is piano exams. Our esteemed forefathers in 19th century London created an examination system that continues to this day to be the international standard for assessing student ability. Whilst piano exams can be an important part of learning music, they can also (and quickly) turn students off learning when taught using a traditional approach.

Today, exams have about 50% retention of students from grade to grade. That means for every 100 students participating in a Grade 1 exam, around 1 student will make it to grade 8. It's a tragedy and yet across society, musical ability is often judged by a student's highest examination performance level. It is understandable because this system is structured and has been in place for well over 100 years.

What if we were able to take the piano exam repertoire and teach it using a non-traditional approach so that the student listened, moved, danced, and sang before playing the music? What if teachers related the harmony in the exam pieces to that of the contemporary music students listen to? What if students listened and watched video recordings and backing tracks before even touching their instrument?

These ideas are all part of the courses that I have written for piano teachers who want to empower their students with musical skills that will last a lifetime and prepare their students for exams. It's a win-win! Teachers and students can have better outcomes and we can significantly increase the odds of children surviving their journey to continue as adult music makers. We can improve on 1 in 100 students surviving. It doesn't matter whether it's ABRSM, Trinity College, AMEB, ANZCA, RCM, MTB, NZMEB, it's all about how you teach.

Mistakes are to learn from, just like spilt juice was a catalyst for me entering this world of music teaching.

Author Bio:

Paul Myatt is a passionate piano teacher, performer, author, course writer, and workshop presenter. Paul is co-founder of the 27-year-old *Forte Music School* network with nearly 8,000 students in Australia, New Zealand, UK & US, and *Piano Teaching Success*.

pianoteachingsuccess.com

THE MUZIE METHODOLOGY

Sam Reti
United States

"I WOULD TEACH CHILDREN MUSIC, PHYSICS, AND PHILOSOPHY; but most importantly music, for the patterns in music and all the arts are the keys to learning"- Plato

Have you ever taught an online music lesson? You know exactly what we are trying to solve then. When the pandemic hit in 2020, music teachers found themselves in a very unfortunate position. Little focus was being placed on music education and thousands of students stopped taking lessons. We saw a problem that needed to be addressed and were in a unique position to help.

I've personally spoken with hundreds of music teachers across the country and globally. They had such limited resources available to them for their specific industry. Fatigued or frustrated, is the main emotion most music teachers felt after a day of teaching virtually. Either there were annoying sound issues, bad connections, or the students were not as engaged in their lessons. Nor were the tools being provided for business meetings created for music education. Yet these platforms were still seen as staples to provide online music lessons. I realized that there was a better way to teach online by providing technology that could create an environment so engaging, students would ask to stay online permanently.

Muzie.Live started in 2019 as an on-demand marketplace. Think Uber for music teachers, you could hop online any time and take incoming lesson requests, get paid by the minute, and work on your own schedule. The hope was that teachers would be able to have a new avenue of flexible income while providing easily accessible high-quality education to students around the world.

It sounded great, but when we launched the initial beta in January of 2020, almost every teacher that signed up asked if they could also host their own students. As schools were closing and the pandemic became more serious, teachers needed resources to adapt. We had the technology to host online lessons and now there was a pressing need and high demand for it but in a different way than we could have ever imagined.

In less than two weeks, we completely changed our business model to support the needs of our growing teacher community. We went from hosting on-demand lessons to building out a dedicated virtual music studio. Over the course of our first year, we developed a full suite of music course tools, in and outside the lesson, to create engaged students and organized teachers. This was only possible through listening to what our users needed and a desire to provide something truly special for both teachers and students alike. As the pandemic progressed, we continued to adapt to teachers needs from online innovation to hybrid and in-person lesson solutions. There have been many challenges and obstacles along the way, especially with just my dad and I running the entirety of the business together.

Enhancing music education across the world has always been a dream of mine since I can remember. If you would have told me on my very first day of Berklee College of Music this is how I would be doing it, with my dad by my side, I wouldn't have believed you. I would have probably told you that I planned on being just like him though, a rockstar. My dad, a touring drummer in the '80s in England, opened for some of the legends such as *Black Sabbath* and *Iron Maiden*. Today, he is an extremely talented and accomplished software developer. Together, we designed and built *Muzie.Live* from the ground up along with suggestions from our community of music teachers.

I still remember this specific moment, about three or four months into beta and the pandemic, a teacher messaged in a photo of their six-year-old student's music notebook. He had drawn the *Muzie.Live* logo on the front. At this moment, my dad and I thought we couldn't have been prouder of what we had accomplished together. Almost two years in, those moments have never stopped coming. Being able to work alongside music educators around the world to make a positive impact in the music education of thousands of students has been indescribably rewarding. With this impact, we strive to not just provide technology but a course methodology, mindset. and community for an interactive teaching philosophy dedicated to engaging lessons. Even after hundreds and hundreds of demos, it is still the most exciting and rewarding part of my day when the teacher has what I like to call the aha moment. It's almost like they are finally seeing the light at the end of a long dark tunnel and all the possibilities that come with it.

Muzie.Live has grown from just one teacher outside of Boston, Massachusetts to teachers in over forty countries, with customer support chats at three in the morning, many days on end spent in the office, and never-ending back-to-back demo days. It is worth it when I hear teachers are not only able to sustain their businesses on and offline but continuously grow their studios with students in and out of their area. Or even better, when I get feedback from students saying how much they love their online lessons now. Creating this course platform has been the most challenging, rewarding, and most incredible experience of my life. From the Reti family to all our Muzie teachers and students, we promise to continue to build upon our Muzie Methodology to bring you the best and most innovative lesson experience.

Author Bio:

Sam Reti is the founder of *Muzie.Live*, a guitar teacher, course creator, and musician. Sam has been designing and building music education software with his dad, since graduating from Berklee college of music in 2016.

http://www.Muzie.Live

TURNING YOUR DISABILITY INTO YOUR SUPERPOWER

Shelagh McKibbon-U'Ren
Canada

DO YOU EVER SECOND GUESS YOURSELF? DO YOU EVER NEED TO check it thrice, not just twice, to make certain that you did it correctly? Do you ever say something completely different from what you meant to say? If so, welcome to my world.

I have learning disabilities. I am dyslexic. I process things differently. I struggle memorizing. I mix numbers and letters up. I have anxiety. But it feels so negative to call these my 'disabilities'. I call them my 'Superpowers'.

My Superpowers mean that:

I need to see instructions one step at a time.

I need to process instructions one step at a time.

I need to have Memory Joggers - word or picture associations.

I need to be reassured that I am doing things correctly.

I need to learn outside of the box.

As a piano teacher, my Superpowers mean that I need to study a piece myself before I feel comfortable teaching it. The longer the piece, the more I need to break it down and analyze the sections. I have a music library full of 'teacher's copy' books – music that I have written all kinds of teaching notes in. Because the brain pathway/connection between what I see and what I do/say/play is often discombobulated, I often use CD recordings and YouTube to verify that I am playing the note names correctly.

Comparing what I see with what I hear other performers do reassures me that I am teaching the music correctly. When I don't do that, I second guess myself on whether or not I actually read (then played) the notes correctly.

Believe me, having an adjudicator point out that I taught the Menuet playing a G instead of an E at Measure 6 is a total downer. Sure, I may have taught everything else correctly – dynamics, articulation, musicality. But missing that one note makes me feel like a total failure. Not only do my Superpowers affect my piano playing and teaching, but they also affect how I learn and teach Theory.

For every Theory workbook and Practice Exam I have ever taught, I had to purchase the books and write in every single answer myself. It drove me crazy that there were no answer books for me to check my answers with.

For years, I marked theory by looking to see if there was anything different between my answers in my 'Teacher's Copy' and my student's answer. If they were different, then I had to figure out whether I had made the mistake or whether my student had answered the question incorrectly.

It was so frustrating. How was I to know what I didn't know if I couldn't check an answer book to see whether or not I answered it correctly? When answer books for theory started to become available, they didn't look at all like the workbook. Talk about sending my learning disabilities, I mean my Superpowers, into a tailspin. I struggled to match a list of answers with the actual corresponding questions in the workbook.

Then, in 2008, I discovered the *Ultimate Music Theory Workbooks*. These workbooks had matching answer books that looked exactly like the workbook. I was beyond excited! I ordered them all – the *Ultimate Music Theory Basic, Intermediate* and *Advance Workbooks* and their matching answer books.

I worked through these workbooks and then I marked them with the answer books. When something didn't match between my workbook and the answer book, I could figure it out before I had to teach it. I finally started to feel confident teaching theory.

I loved these six books so much that I began to correspond with the author, Glory St. Germain. God's timing was perfect – Glory needed an Editor for her next printing, and I knew that, with a few little changes, these Theory workbooks could work with all students, including those with special learning needs like me. Glory and I still laugh at the first email I sent her with my suggestions. It was fourteen pages long and only covered my ideas for the *Basic Rudiments Workbook*.

In 2013, after writing the *Prep 1, Prep 2*, and *Complete Rudiments Workbooks* and answer books together, Glory invited me to write the *Ultimate Music Theory Exam Series*. This was so exciting. I knew that I needed to craft an Exam Course that would support and encourage students of all learning styles, including those with Superpowers. And every exam would have a matching answer exam so that no other teacher had to second guess whether or not they were answering correctly.

The *Ultimate Music Theory Exam Course* has sixteen books. For the Preparatory, Basic, Intermediate and Advanced Levels, there are two exam books – Set 1 and Set 2 – with four exams in each book. There are matching answer books too.

In each exam book, the first 2 exams have *UMT* Tips for

every question. These are memory joggers that helped me and my students to stay on track when answering the questions.

When you have Superpowers like me, it is not easy to remember everything all the time. By seeing these tips, I wanted other eachers and students to realize that it was okay to need reminders. If you don't remember the steps required to get the answer, then go back and review. This exam series is a tool to build confidence before you have to write a final exam.

When working with the *Ultimate Music Theory Certification Course*, I realized that there were other teachers like me who also needed to write out their Memory Joggers before they opened the exam. (Seriously – I remember completing my RCM Advanced Rudiments Exam and totally brain-farting over which came first in the staff – the Key Signature or the Time Signature.) So, we created the *UMT "MAP* – "Making Achievement Possible" – for each Level. These MAPS are now a part of our Teacher Training Course Materials. Teachers can show their students how to write out a simple Memory Jogger Sheet that will support successful completion of each exam.

Looking back over my 40+ years as a teacher, I am proud that I have turned my learning disabilities into Superpowers. It is okay to learn differently from others. How have your Superpowers changed your learning or your teaching? If you feel stuck – like you can't do it – then look for ways and opportunities to turn that feeling around. You can do it!

Author Bio:

Shelagh McKibbon-URen UMTC is the author of the *Ultimate Music Theory Exam Series Course*, *UMT* Examiner and the Editor for *Ultimate Music Theory*. Shelagh teaches piano, Theory, Voice, History & Harmony. Her favorite role is Maw-Maw to her two grandchildren.

www.UltimateMusicTheory.com

THE PODCASTING MUSICIAN

Dr. Heidi Kay Begay
United States

IF GIVEN THE TIME AND THE RIGHT AMOUNT OF ENERGY, MOST creative projects have a way of evolving into their ultimate form.

The creative project that evolved, for me, was my digital baby, which is called the *Flute 360 Podcast*. This podcast started as my thesis for my Doctoral of Musical Arts degree from Texas Tech University (2018), to a glorified hobby, to a C.V. builder, and lastly as a marketing arm for my music-based business. When I started the podcast in March of 2018, I never imagined that I would connect with thousands of flutists at the global level, nor would I create an income through the platform but here we are. Throughout the life of the podcast, I have grown with the platform in more ways than one. I have matured as a person, educator, businesswoman, and musician. Since you, the reader, are most likely a musician, I would like to shed some light on the growth I experienced as a podcasting musician. The number of parallels between podcasting and music-making are numerous.

Some of these similarities include a deeper understanding of the creative course process, choosing repertoire or content wisely, the art of recording, dynamic communicative skills, the art of listening, and lastly – not only finding your unique voice – but embracing it. I will not explore all these learned lessons in detail; however, I will highlight the last two.

First, the art of listening is the biggest lesson that I have grasped as a podcast host. To truly listen to what my guest and audience are saying was life-changing for me. Passive listening is quite different from engaged listening. To truly hear their voice and their message was a turning point for the relationships in my personal and business life. In addition, this newly discovered art of listening extended into the practice room. To hear the voice of the instrument, composer, and my artistic voice together completely took my playing to a new musical level. Second, finding and embracing my creative voice was another well-learned lesson. While in school, I was a devoted student to my music studies. I studied music theory, history, and my instrument feverishly. Because I cared about my grades, I approached my music juries and recitals with the wrong mindset. My main desire was to appease the jury by playing all the right notes at the correct time, which is respectable, but it suffocated my musical voice. I found myself sucked into the black-and-white, which was on the music stand, instead of singing through my instrument. My loving teachers had difficulty getting me to play from within and expressing myself as an artist.

When I hear myself say these words out loud, it is even hard for me to comprehend a musician who did not know how to express herself through her instrument. Music to me was math and science. I was not expressing feelings or a story. And because of this, my connection to the music and my audience suffered. Until podcasting. Podcasting permitted me to find my creative voice and to learn how to communicate what I felt and knew at the internal level. Podcasting lovingly forced me to get off the page. Yes, I could type out the script of the episode, but how would that help me to connect with my audience if I sounded robotic? By outlining my episode's main points and relaying these ideas into a microphone, I was able to strengthen my communicative skills and find my creative voice. I was willing to take risks as a public speaker and establish an intimate connection with my listener.

Whether you are a recording artist, composer, or performing artist, take this lesson back into your relationship with the music. Understanding the musical context, theory, and the form of the composition is a must. However, after practicing, you are then ready to share the music with your audience. To deliver an impactful performance, one must get off the page and connect with the listener at the human level. To be comfortable in your creative voice and clearly (and convincingly) communicate your musical thoughts is the heart of music.

At the same time, as I was maturing as a performing artist, I noticed how *Flute 360* was continually bringing me new career opportunities. These profitable opportunities were only possible because of the podcast. Due to my personal and business transformation, it was clear to me that I must share this knowledge with the music world. Therefore, *The Podcasting Musician* class was born.

In August of 2020, I met a talented young woman who sought guidance about her playing and music business. From our conversation, it was clear to me that by her producing her music-based podcast it would not only help her musicality soar but her business, too!

To help her strategically, I had to design a course curriculum that we could follow together. I decided to take the foundation of my DMA thesis and turn it into a five-week remote course. Talk about creative projects that undergo an evolution!

The intent of *The Podcasting Musician* is to help musicians build their podcasts from scratch to launch in just five weeks. Within these five weeks, I guide the musician through creating the podcast theme, learning the ins and outs of recording, editing the audio, creating content, the art of interviewing, marketing the show, and monetizing through their podcast.

Yes, the class covers the logistics of podcasting, but as stated earlier, it is much more than that. It is giving musicians a digital space to learn about their creative selves, and at the same time, using their podcast as a marketing arm for their business.

Once the musician completes the class, they then have a piece of digital real estate. Within their newly designed digital home, they have the foundation laid for their creative and entrepreneurial worlds to scale to a whole new level. If podcasting can help transform another musician's creative and entrepreneurial world like it did for me, then *The Podcasting Musician* is considered a success in my book.

Author Bio:

Dr. Heidi Kay Begay is a flutist, educator, course creator, and podcaster. In 2018, Heidi created the *Flute 360* podcast, and since its inception, it has published 165 episodes and has received 53,000 downloads from 70 countries.

https://heidikaybegay.com/thepodcastingmusician/

IRMTNZ TEACHER TRAINING COURSES

Wendy Hunt
New Zealand

INSTITUTE OF REGISTERED MUSIC TEACHERS OF NEW Zealand (IRMTNZ) Teacher Training Courses - Why?

I'm sure we've all experienced the brilliant mathematician who could not get us to learn algebra, or the great poet who couldn't help us craft the perfect rhyming couplet, or the famous artist who couldn't get us to paint anything remotely realistic.

Performance skill is quite separate from teaching skill, yet how many performers resort to teaching to earn a living? This is a common state for university students – teaching a few beginners 'on the side' to help pay study fees, but the chances of frustration - for both teacher and pupil – can be high.

Observing how beautifully infants in so many cultural communities around the world learn at the side of a family member who knows them, loves them, and patiently supports them, one wonders how society came to accept that the fantastic concert pianist who lives in the neighbourhood will be the best teacher for our children.

There are many adults in our communities who learnt for a few years then gave up – yet few who regret this decision. These people share horror stories of crabby teachers inflicting harsh teaching methods - stories that would terrify a youngster today.

Resilience, now more than ever, needs to be nurtured in our children. Careers can change several times in a lifetime, so the need to develop many skills is paramount.

Give a child a fish you feed him for a day. Teach a child to fish you feed him for life - Chinese Proverb.

The New Zealand Ministry of Education (MOE) embraces these Key Competencies as essential skills to focus on while teaching a specific subject, in order to develop life skills:

- Thinking about our thinking
- Relating to others
- Understanding language, symbols, and text
- Managing ourselves
- Participating and contributing.

Such competencies can be developed through a rich music education programme, growing self-smart, people-smart, word-smart, number-smart, body-smart, picture-smart, nature-smart citizens. MOE also integrates collaborative learning methods into the curriculum delivery, encouraging communication, respect, and teamwork.

With a balance of these skills our young people are better equipped to face an uncertain future with confidence and creative, critical thinking.

Let him sit with the problem for a while and solve it himself. Let him know nothing because you have told him but because he has learnt it for himself. Let the children discover - Rousseau.

Our Inspiration

Absorbing Francis Bacon's declaration, "Wonder is the seed of knowledge" and Suzuki's books, *Nurtured by Love* and *Ability Development from Age Zero*, it became increasingly obvious that child-centred learning methods needed to be developed. This includes how children like to perceive, think, move, practice, work independently or in partnership, and solve puzzles as well as the most appropriate age to start learning.

Perhaps no more the old habit of thinking that at age seven it's time to get the tonsils out, start Brownies, swimming, ballet and music lessons.

Rather, feel as the child does, understanding their individual level of wonder and development:

- Begin as early as possible
- Create the best possible environment
- Use the finest teaching methods
- Provide a great deal of training
- Use the finest teachers
- Overcoming Obstacles and Challenges

Further adages such as 'if you always do what you've always done, you'll always get what you've always got' and 'you reap what you sow' continued to resonate, particularly as we surveyed our members regularly and found a trend of ageing teachers and lessening interest in developing new professional skills.

The majority of our members were middle aged women, mostly piano, violin and singing teachers, perhaps unwittingly reinforcing the image of a formal, autocratic method. We also wanted to attract younger teachers, diverse ethnicities, genres, and instruments, to be inclusive of all types of music and musicians. To expect teachers to attend a training course away from work and their families, however, was unrealistic: asking them to produce hypothetical essays seemed equally unrealistic.

It was clear that to authentically 'walk our talk' as engaged and engaging educators we needed to develop a training course that allowed for flexibility of presentation style, content, and submission date. It was also clear that for our professional organisation to survive, we needed to continually strive for relevance in the changing world.

Consequently, while study and the practical assignments of our courses do follow a prescription (so IRMTNZ can be accountable for the skills graduates will gain) candidates are encouraged to relate them immediately to their current pupil(s) and teaching situation.

Learning is via e-platform discussion and regular video forums, recorded webinars, reading, and regular discussion with a personally assigned mentor in the participant's hometown. There is also a one-day Contact Workshop applying all the learning so far and acknowledging the overwhelming power of personal contact. Feedback is swift and encouraging, suggesting future steps for improved expedience so that young teachers work smarter, not harder, thus giving them more time and energy to engage with the pupil at their side.

We have also opened up a segment of the course to established teachers, so they can upskill and explore modern methods, terminology, and resources that will relate to the changing and increasingly diverse styles of learners.

The courses have been segmented into various levels of learner-ability so as not to drown the trainee teacher in too many ideas at once. In line with current achievement and assessment practice in schools, assignments are graded as Not Achieved (with a chance to improve and resubmit after support), Achieved, Merit and Excellence. Conveniently these initial assessment grades link with a student-self-assessment of Novice, Apprentice, Master and Expert and can help frame both individual and collaborative learning experiences.

Trainee teachers are encouraged to instil a practice of self-review and pupil-review in their lessons whereby the communication lies open and honest, the learning is relevant and personalised, the learning process is based on a team approach with teacher, pupil and parent participating and contributing, and the direction for independent practice and the next week's goal is a SMART one:

- Small steps
- Measurable
- Achievable
- Relevant
- Time-framed

Since establishing our Teacher Training Courses, the Teaching Council of Aotearoa New Zealand has engaged IRMTNZ in providing a similar re-training/refreshment course for specialist music teachers who have left the school system for myriad reasons. Our Teacher Education Refresh (TER) Course empowers and updates the training, again in a practical, relevant, and energising way so that these specialists may re-enter the school system and provide our learners with the best quality music education.

We are looking ahead to a resurgence of quality, energy, and achievement in our music education.

Author Bio:

Wendy Hunt FIRMT M.ED DIP TCHG. LTCL

Wendy taught from pre-school through to tertiary before opening a private music studio. She delivers Teacher Training Courses and performs as accompanist, chorister, conductor, and jazz keyboardist.

www.learnmusicnz.org.nz

A MUSICAL DREAM TEAM

Alessandra DiCienzo
Canada

WHEN REBECCA GOODE AND I, ALESSANDRA DICIENZO, FIRST met over fifteen years ago, we just clicked. I would describe us as musical soul mates if such a thing exists. Rebecca and I both love anything piano: piano music, piano teaching, piano playing, piano conferences, piano concerts, you get the idea. Not too long after we met, we had a conversation lamenting the fact that we were always so busy with family life and teaching we never found enough time to play for ourselves.

This conversation led to a piano duo partnership that got us back to doing what we love most, making music at the piano. Now, to be quite honest, most of our practice time together started with a sincere effort to work on our piano duo music but would often meander into discussions about our teaching, our students, our successes, and our failures. However, through these monthly exchanges, we realized that we had similar philosophies when it came to our teaching and approaches to our students.

We would share our teaching ideas, discuss the best ways to approach a piece or technical passage, brainstorm ways to get our students engaged in practicing, and everything in between. One of the topics of conversation which would constantly surface was teaching beginner students. These conversations eventually led to the idea for our course book series *Take Off! With Technique*.

Working with beginner students is a rewarding yet challenging process. Many readers will agree that the first two years of a young student's piano journey are crucial for the development of good playing and practice habits. Most teachers will use a beginner piano method book series to facilitate this process when working with beginner piano students. In our monthly meetups, Rebecca and I felt the need to create a course book that would progressively take students through technical requirements while instilling some fundamental playing skills. We felt these were best achieved in a setting by rote so that students could learn to watch and feel how to effectively execute technical exercises. Then, when the skills are achieved with some degree of success, students could apply the technique to the pieces they are working on. By learning technique by rote, students can really focus on hand position and tone production. Rebecca and I wanted to create a course which offered beginners the opportunity to experience technique with freedom, relaxation, and creative activities in the book.

To take on a project of this size was at times exciting and invigorating and other times it was a struggle and frustrating. We spent a full year trying out our ideas with our students, and we each kept a notebook near us while we taught. We jotted down any inspirational thoughts that came to us while we were teaching and made notes about what ideas were working, as well as what we thought needed tweaking and what ideas were a bust. The time spent on this phase of our project was important as it revealed to us how certain aspects of the book should be organized on the page, and it gave us a sense of presentation order for each technique element. We spent a considerable amount of time and thought to ensure that the book was accessible to beginners of all types of abilities, so each lesson contains extra exercises and bonus ideas. Although the books were designed with a younger student in mind, they have also worked successfully for older students.

A project of this size was easier to tackle working as a team. One thing to consider if you are working with a partner is to make sure that you are comfortable giving honest feedback to that person and accepting honest feedback in turn. Sometimes you must hear, "This idea is not working," and you can't take it personally. There must be an element of trust between you and your partner where you can feel free to offer any ideas or suggestions without fear of judgement or fear that your partner will become upset. The plus side of working with a partner is that you have another perspective at all times. It is easy to get caught up in your own idea or mode of thinking, so it is helpful to have another voice to either reaffirm the path you are on or to show a new slant that you never considered. The workload with a partner is also much easier to manage as tasks can be delegated making the project seem less daunting overall.

Rebecca and I are firmly (and happily) entrenched in all things piano related, and both of our educations are rooted in musical study, so it comes as no surprise that we faced certain challenges when it came to the business aspect of marketing and promoting our course books. In today's world, one must rely heavily on digital tools for marketing and promotion. With our family commitments and busy work schedules, it has been difficult to find the time to maintain a constant online presence.

Rebecca and I thrive on live workshop presentations and talking directly with teachers, so we try to focus on this aspect. We find it difficult to balance our commitments to teaching, and other musical pursuits, and the time and energy needed for digital marketing. However, we are always looking at finding ways of promoting our books that complement who we are because we are excited to share our course ideas with others. So, what is our big Why? The simple answer is to help our students. Our books started from asking and discussing questions that we had no answer to. Why is beginner technique often presented through pieces? How can we have beginner students creatively exploring the whole piano with their technique? Where can we find an easy-to-follow curriculum for beginner technique?

Rebecca and I felt that our students would greatly benefit from a book of this nature, and we are glad that it has helped other teachers and their students as well. To have realized our vision and to see students succeeding in our course with our books is very satisfying. If you have a vision of something you would like to do or create, we encourage you to go for it. Even if you affect the life of one teacher or student, you will have made a difference.

Author Bio:

Alessandra DiCienzo and Rebecca Goode are course creators and musicians from Niagara Falls, Ontario, Canada. They are passionate about teaching and are the authors of *Take Off! With Technique.*

www.takeoffwithtechnique.com

WHY I CREATED "THE UNIVERSE OF MUSIC"

Dr. Marcin Bela
Poland/USA

MY NAME IS MARCIN BELA; I'M A COMPOSER, PERFORMER, course creator, and educator born and raised in Krakow, Poland and currently based in 'Music City USA' - Nashville, TN. I've had a diverse career, spanning many genres, from classical to rock n roll, world, and electronica. Getting to know such remote corners of the musical universe allowed me to understand the deeply archetypal patterns all musical genres have in common, and I always loved sharing those observations with my students.

But I didn't create *The Universe of Music* (a course presenting musical concepts through analogies with math, science, and language) just to offer another approach to music theory. Rather, I wanted to use music theory to inspire a personal and spiritual change in how families facilitate learning.

My father didn't wait for the school to teach me about atoms, trees, and stars. He was just too excited to share what he knew and wanted to inspire in me the awe that fueled his own relentless hunger for knowledge.

As a private music teacher, I get to witness how families handle their children's education firsthand. And it saddens me that the norm in the American mainstream is to let the schools lead the way because that means that the children's discovery of the universe is largely controlled by the heartless bureaucracy of the school systems. I believe that the path of healing is for the parents to reassert their duty and privilege to guide the most important processes in their children's lives: learning.

But how? Already overburdened by the extreme intensity of regular schooling, the last thing the children want is another teacher in their lives. But what if parents presented themselves as fellow students?

That's why I designed *The Universe of Music* as a resource the parents and the children can use together as a bonding exercise of discovery. And while the course can potentially get the students from ground zero to being ready for a freshman music theory class at a university, that's not ultimately the goal. The goal is for parents and children (or teacher and students) to really talk, to imagine things, to contemplate the wonders of nature and music's mechanisms, and to learn something interesting.

Why music theory then? Aren't there more interesting things for families to talk about in their free time? Well, music is not just a mildly curious topic. Music is an inherent component of human life. Your mother's heartbeat was the soundtrack to your life before birth. Perhaps it taught your own heart how to beat. Music is the oldest human language - if by language we mean communication through sonic patterns. In the sense that it transcends semantics, music is similar to mathematics. But because of the physical nature of sound, those abstract patterns become a palpable, time-bound experience, which can bypass the mind and engage directly with feelings and emotions.

And now, thanks to the wireless, on-demand, and portable

reality we live in, music is everywhere, pouring out of every phone, car, and earbud, affecting our attention and emotions, selling products, and starting revolutions. Isn't it useful to know how that world works? Why do some notes sound better together than others? What are notes to begin with? How do composers narrow down the infinity of pattern choices to pick from?

Of course, these are not new thoughts. The wisdom of all eras - from ancient Greek philosophers to modern-age parents - have always considered the knowledge of music a crucial element of a child's education. Control group studies have demonstrated a positive effect of music lessons on children's general academic performance.

But something new, deeper, and even more exciting is happening now, in the 21st century. As the cutting edge of theoretical physics begins to touch fingers with the spiritual teachings of mystics and saints, the New Age vocabulary is entering mainstream culture and a new generation of humans is on the rise, one that will bridge the rational and the intuitive, science, and spirituality.

And that bridge between the two polarities is made of art. Art is the connective chemistry between the seeming opposites of technical and dreamy minds. Science describes how creation works. But creation is, well, creative. It is art; it's the symphony of life: atoms dancing around each other, swapping electrons and forming ever-changing bonds and formations, the same way as notes, motifs, chords, and melodies do. Life is genius and infinite, yet sometimes whimsical and arbitrary, like Haydn's *Surprise Symphony*. God is an artist and playing with art is perhaps the most God-like thing we get to do.

There are these moments in student-teacher relationships that we all live for: the moments when the students get it - they see how a certain mechanism works and how brilliant it is. At that moment, they are gazing deep into the wonder of existence, and you - the teacher - get goosebumps from opening that door for them.

I've had many exciting experiences as a composer and performer of music. But my most cherished moments as a musician have not necessarily been in the brightness of stage lights. My best moments may just be the quiet ones, when I get to contemplate the genius of Music herself, the giant womb of musical "matter" that births songs, symphonies, and soundtracks, just like the physical fabric of existence births amoebas, trees. and planets.

My dad passed away a couple years ago. He was a great man and taught me many wonderful things. But the most valuable gift he left behind in me is my ability to contemplate. To not just file facts in my brain, but to take a moment to admire God for making whatever it is in that, insanely brilliant way. And if my students forget every single last thing about music theory but remember to pause to contemplate the genius of life, I'll consider my work a success.

Author Bio:

Dr. Marcin Bela is a Polish American composer, performer, course creator, and educator whose appearances have spanned the globe and spectrum of genre and style.

www.theuniverseofmusic.com

A NEW PERSPECTIVE MADE ALL THE DIFFERENCE

Shauna Hunter
Canada

WHO AM I? JUST ANOTHER PIANO TEACHER IN A WORLD FULL of piano teachers? Yup. Nothing amazing here. That's what I would tell myself. In fact, I was suffering from 'imposter syndrome'. I managed to teach my students, but I didn't have any credentials hanging on my wall, so I believed I couldn't be anything better than average and maybe shouldn't even be teaching at all. I had been well trained by a Belgian concert pianist but for some reason didn't believe in myself, and I wasn't listening to all the positive feedback I received regularly from friends, family, and students. But, I really wanted a grand piano, which meant I needed to make some money. The only way I was going to be able to pay for it was to teach piano on my old upright. So, I kept on teaching. Yes, I must admit that my motivation was money. I had a modest number of students that was growing each year, but I wasn't sure if I was serving them well.

I felt the need to legitimize my teaching. I discovered the

Royal Conservatory of Music had a teacher certification course. The requirements fell well within my abilities, and I could do it online in my own time. I had attended many of their workshops and felt comfortable in their program. It wasn't long before I had a certificate to hang on my wall. I was certified as a piano teacher for elementary level students. A couple of years later, I got my certification to teach intermediate level students. I also completed the *Ultimate Music Theory* Certification course for teaching music theory. I had credentials. Interestingly, it didn't change how I was teaching. As it turns out, I already knew and was doing all that I needed to be an effective teacher. What it did change was my belief in my ability to teach. My studio began to grow.

Then the universe threw me a curve ball. I was diagnosed with breast cancer. I had to scale back my teaching hours to allow time for treatment. Thankfully, I am well now, and cancer free, but the experience helped me learn some good life lessons. Facing my own mortality forced me to reconsider how I look at life. I learned that life is precious, and we need to spend the hours we have on this earth well. We should do things that make us happy. We should do things that make others happy. So many people served me by giving their time and knowledge to help me that I now feel compelled to help others in any way I can. It forced me to see how priceless each personal relationship is. I listened to music through my time in therapy, and I grew to love it even more and appreciate how beautiful and personal it can be. Music helped to lift my spirits at a time when everything was looking dark and dismal.

That experience changed my perspective. It gave me a new reason to teach. It is no longer about the money or the credentials. It's all about my students, building relationships with them, and teaching in a way that will help them achieve their goals. I consider each individual student and his or her needs. Some of my students have learning disabilities and were progressing very slowly, if at all. They were struggling. Although they loved the music, learning to play it was causing them frustration. I was feeling frustrated because they couldn't pick it up as quickly as my other students. I realized the students were not the problem. I needed to change my approach to suit their learning styles more appropriately.

To serve them better, I spent many hours scouring the internet, gleaning valuable insights and ideas for teaching that will help each child with their individual goals. I connected with music teachers around the world and learned from their success stories. I benefitted from coaching calls that not only help with running my music studio but also help me grow on a personal level. With all I have learned, I have put together a course curriculum and a teaching style that serves both me and my students better. This last year, as I have implemented these new course ideas, I have seen my students grow. Learning has become a little easier and more enjoyable. Those students who were having such a hard time learning the music now have fun learning and leave their lessons smiling. And that makes me happy. I saw such success and growth in these students with learning difficulties that I have carried over the new course methods and ideas to all my students. We are all enjoying the change. All the time and energy spent in researching was well worth it.

I now approach each lesson with love and gratitude. I'm so lucky to spend time with each child who comes into my studio. Their energy and their stories and their love for music uplift me. Money is no longer my primary motivation. I'm teaching because I love the kids and I love the music. It makes me happy to share the knowledge and skills I have with my students so that they, too, can learn to love and appreciate music as much as I do. Maybe one day it will help them through a difficult time, as it did for me with breast cancer. Or maybe it will just enrich their lives as only music can.

Author Bio:

Shauna Hunter UMTC is an *Ultimate Music Theory* Certified Teacher, RCM Certified Teacher and course creator. She teaches piano and music theory, as well as playing both piano and organ. Her passion is helping children learn and grow with an enjoyable, interactive approach. Her favorite things are family, music, and chocolate!

https://www.pianowithshauna.com/

ENRICHING A MUSICAL WORLD THROUGH EBONY AND IVORY

Edy Panjaitan
Indonesia

ALL ALONG MY JOURNEY I BEGAN TO REALIZE HOW MUCH education plays an important part in forming any career in music; indeed, it is through the means of blazing an individual trail that a person becomes able to educate and, ultimately, to inspire.

The journey has taken me through many twists and turns throughout my career, and I have had many great minds leading and molding me as I have progressed.

In the beginning, I remember that becoming a teacher was the furthest thing from my mind, largely because of the responsibilities this role comes with. I finally attended university, reading music and education. I confess I had prior experience as a tutor at school, helping to tutor in junior classes, and teaching them to play keyboards and guitar, and helping them with academic subjects like English and mathematics.

The passion really began when I was in my second year of

the music degree, and I took charge of my own learning process. I took on part-time jobs as a music teacher and taught piano to young students. There was much I learned at this point in my life, and this really helped me hone my skills; I began to understand more about the importance of education in music. I strongly believe the present Z generation is attracted to many different influences, and I found around my community that music is becoming more and more of an essential part in overall education.

Parents are increasingly concerned with musical education for their young children. One of many special memories was when I was teaching a beginner, who at the time was four years old. He was the youngest student I had ever taught up to that point. After a few months of study, I was surprised at his rapid progress, and I suggested to his parents that he should participate in festivals or competitions. After around a year of study, I entered him into a competition. Because of his hard work and perseverance, he attained both diamond and platinum prizes in that competition. Without the influence of his parents, this would not have been possible. I am so incredibly grateful that his parents were there every step of the way.

It is important to encourage students so that they become increasingly confident. My feeling has always been that performance and/or demonstration is such an important part of the learning process. It is clear to me that students are motivated when they can express themselves in music through performing. These students were able to prove themselves during international music examinations. My pride as a teacher came from observing this gradual growth. I became more interested in pedagogy and performance. When all these things fell into place, I knew deep down that I would strive to be a professional piano teacher.

It is my desire to help these young individuals succeed in every possible way. For this to happen, I must create an environment that supports the students in many ways. The environment must be safe, support risk-taking, and invite the sharing of ideas from all individuals. I must create an atmosphere in which a student can grow and mature musically, intellectually, socially, emotionally, and physically. I am excited to be able to contribute my strengths and proficiency to the process. As an extroverted and personable communicator with a proven track record in directing performances, conducting lessons, and in lecturing, my focus is always on building strong professional relationships, and this has been an invaluable asset throughout my career.

Throughout this long journey, I finally established my own piano school and came up with my own personal approach, binding my interests with my study in the city of the 'home of the Giant Panda', Chengdu, China. This was an inspirational time for me in this culturally vibrant city. I founded the *Panda Piano Course* in July 2020, an unpredictable time, and so encouraged me to set up virtual piano lessons.

In the future, we aim to set up a studio to help physically shape the nature of these lessons. Our *Panda Piano Course* enables students to develop skills and experiences they need to progress along their own musical journeys. This course is a space where students and instructors alike can thrive and make the most of their talents. We provide high quality, affordable, online piano lessons, peppered with masterclasses delivered by international experts from around the world. This is the perfect course for students to enrich their musical knowledge, musicianship, performing skills, and help to achieve their own personal goals. With these affordable online lessons, we welcome passionate students from all around the world.

At present the *Panda Piano Course* is developing a unique syllabus while incorporating existing teaching methods. Our faculty members are highly experienced on the international performing stage and have produced successful piano students both in their native countries and across the globe. With every lesson they teach, they bring their rich experience, knowledge, inspiration, and passion.

Our hashtag vibe is 'Abundant in Harmony', best represented by the color of the panda, with ebony and ivory, we intend to create perfect harmony together, studying in an environment of diversity, expressing our own musical voice, with messages of peace, love, and sincerity from the international community. In the same way that bamboo grows leaves, so too are the skills, techniques, and knowledge that we deliver.

The cane widens as we progress through stages. The metaphorical panda nurtures the bamboo, and when the skill is mastered, it consumes the leaves. *Panda Piano Course* provides online events, including 'panda piano corner' #theworldmusical-sharinginspiration and is designed with piano students, piano teachers, and music lovers in mind. We host numerous different international speakers from all over the world who wish to share their knowledge, motivation, and experiences, answering specific questions you may have. On our website there are places where visitors can read blogs, shop for merchandise, and even donate to help support our program. We do really hope that *Panda Piano Course* will be music to everyone's ears and be a useful contribution to the global music community. Jia-you!

Author Bio:

Edy Rapika Panjaitan is the Founder & CEO of Panda Piano Course - high quality online piano lessons and guidance master-classes with international experts. Edy is a music educator, course creator, lecturer, pianist, arranger, composer, music educator, lecturer, and international best-selling-author.

.

https://pandapianocourse.com

ONE GLIMMER OF HOPE BECAME THE ULTIMATE SUCCESS STORY

Glory St. Germain
Canada

ONE GLIMMER OF HOPE IS ALL I WAS LOOKING FOR. A SIMPLE flicker to let me know I was headed in the right direction. Learning music theory is one thing but knowing how to teach music theory effectively is another thing. I know because I learned the hard way.

When my eight-year-old daughter Sherry received a music theory scholarship in the gifted youth program at the University of Manitoba, I was so excited to observe how the theory class was taught so I could help her with her homework. The excitement quickly turned to despair. As a professional teacher, I was disturbed as I noticed the short abrupt tone in the teacher's voice and the strict discipline of how the concepts were presented. The students simply sat attentively, each at their own desks, like little statues, listening carefully, and yet somehow unengaged.

I had to remain silent, this was not my class to teach, even though I felt the urge to ask questions about how music theory was applicable to the sound of the music itself. Why were the children just memorizing terms and analysis? There was no discussion, no listening to music, no fun. I am not sure the word fun was part of the curriculum, and it was evident to me, this was not the way I wanted to teach theory.

As I began teaching music theory, I knew I wanted to teach it differently, passionately, and in a fun and memorable way. And so, I began writing my *Ultimate Music Theory Workbooks* with the Basic, Intermediate, and Advanced Rudiments. I received an email from a passionate educator Shelagh McKibbon-U'Ren who asked if she could send me a few suggestions about my books. I said yes, absolutely. After many pages of notes, she became my editor, then the co-author of the *Ultimate Music Theory Supplemental Series*, and author of the *Ultimate Music Theory Exam Series Course*. Together we've written over fifty books in the *Ultimate Music Theory Program*.

As I traveled around North America presenting teacher workshops, I noticed one common thread wherever I went. When I looked at the teachers' faces as we talked about music theory, there seemed to be a slight wavering of light, but not a shining sparkle of enthusiasm about the topic of teaching theory.

I had a faint vision of all these teachers simply teaching music theory the way my daughter was taught. After all, you are supposed to be learning theory and not having fun, right? Wrong. Yes, you are supposed to learn, but when you engage in fun activities, you learn faster. That's why I became a teacher and a course creator. I am passionate about helping teachers learn how to teach music theory with systems and strategies that can have a powerful impact on musicians of all ages. I thought, there must be a better way to help teachers teach music theory with confidence, purpose, and ultimately joy. I did not want to see the reflection of what I observed in my daughter's theory class. I wanted to take this glimmer of hope, this faintly shining

star, and let it sparkle, glisten, and shimmer like Beethoven's
Moonlight Sonata - it was time to take all these twinkling lights
and create the *Ultimate Music Theory Certification Course* for
teachers.

I remember the day like it was yesterday. I was attending a
teachers' workshop with approximately fifty teachers. The topic
of music theory came up and no one was excited about it. Then
the light bulb went on in my head. I had a bright idea. What if I
could help these teachers become passionate about teaching
music theory? I quickly grabbed a blank piece of paper and
announced that I was creating the *Ultimate Music Theory Certification Course* for teachers and if anyone was interested, please
write your name, phone number, and email on the page. It will
be starting in ninety days. I had not written one word of this
course, perhaps my bright idea was not so bright. But I was
passionate about helping teachers. My goal was to have five or
six teachers sign up out of this group of fifty educators. I had
twenty-seven teachers sign up. Wow, I was in complete shock.

That first live event of twenty-seven music teachers wanting
to learn how to teach music theory more effectively in a fun and
engaging way, put me on the path to writing my success story.
Shelagh wrote the certification course exams and that little
sparkle turned into rippling waves. Shelagh and I traveled from
coast to coast across Canada and the USA presenting the *Ultimate Music Theory Certification Course* as a live event. It was a huge
success.

But there was one more thing that was missing. The ability
for music teachers around the world to have access to the *Ultimate Music Theory Certification Course* without traveling to North
America. And then it happened. Shelagh and I have a regular
writing camp every year as we continue to write books, update
materials, etc., and we said, why not create an online course so
teachers around the world can access this wonderful program.

Writing scripts, hiring a video production company, creating
worksheets, shooting videos, editing, setting up lights, cameras,

writing exams, creating certificates, etc. was a massive undertaking that all started with a simple glimmer of hope. A glimmer of hope that there would be something for teachers that would light them up in teaching music theory, an essential part of all musicians' education.

That glimmer of hope turned into the *Ultimate Success Story* - the international online *Ultimate Music Theory Certification*, that has expanded into the *UMTC Elite Educator Program* along with the *UMT Teachers Membership* where I facilitate weekly group coaching calls, plus articles and worksheets by Shelagh, and games designed by UMT Certified Teacher Joanne Barker - part of our growing UMT Dream Team.

When you have a faint manifestation or indication of what you truly want to accomplish something, make a difference, craft a course, or simply teach more effectively and take your teaching to the next level - then sparkle like a So-La, yes, So-La is part of the UMT Program, and explore how you can implement the mindset, strategies, and tools to grow your teaching business while enriching lives through music education.

Teach with Passion.

Go to UltimateMusicTheory.com to get your Free Ultimate Music Theory Teachers Guide - so you can discover the 5 Proven Teaching Techniques and implement them into your teaching and discover your Why.

Author Bio:

Glory St. Germain, International Bestselling Author, 50+ *Ultimate Music Theory Books, The Power of WHY Series,* and Host of Global Music Summits. Glory is the creator of the *UMT Certification Course, UMTC Elite Educator Program,* and *UMT Teachers Membership* and is an Expert Music Business Coach.

https://UltimateMusicTheory.com/

THANK YOU FOR READING. I, GLORY ST. GERMAIN, HOPE YOU enjoyed this book. Before you go, reviews really help authors, so if you would like to review it on your favourite online book platform or store website, I, and the other contributors would love to hear from you.

AFTERWORD

THE MAGIC OF A SMILE

Glory St. Germain

The magic of a smile began for me on the snowy Christmas Day that I was born. Tears of joy filled my mother's eyes as I opened mine to see her smile for the first time.

It was a party to remember. In fact, my mother named me Glory the Party Queen.

It would be my mother Rosabel's *simple smile* that would guide me through the most challenging times in my life.

By the age of 16, I became an entrepreneur and opened my own piano teaching studio. As my passion for music grew, so did my desire to grow my business. What was holding me back? I felt like I was not good enough, not smart enough and no one wants to learn from a loser.

My mother would smile and say, "Party Queen, you can do anything."

Throughout my life, those words continue to sing in my head "you can do anything" if you learn the one word my mother used to teach me 5 Powerful Lessons: P A R T Y.

P – Process Plan to Success

A process plan is a sequence of planning steps you need to take to develop a guide on how to achieve your goals. It outlines the activities required as well as accessing a constant review of improvement steps needed for continuous growth.

Develop a process plan, a proven step-by-step system to help you not only survive but thrive in the enjoyment of learning and achieving your highest level of excellence.

A – Attitude to Positivity

Attitude is everything. Not only did my mother teach me this lesson, but I also studied Napoleon Hill's book *Success Through a Positive Mental Attitude* (PMA).

The PMA philosophy is having an optimistic disposition in every situation in your life which attracts positive changes and increases achievement. PMA, gratitude, and openness to grow, will magically attract powerful opportunities into your life. Your dreams can become a reality when you have a positive mental attitude.

R – Relationships to Impact

One of life's most precious gifts is our relationships with family, friends, community, clients, and most importantly, ourselves.

Our self-talk"of negativity can destroy our dreams, but only if we let it.

One day I walked into my mother's powder room where she did her hair and makeup. The mirror hanging on the wall was filled with self-talk sticky notes that read:

Smile for 10 minutes to practice your best smile.

Smile to impact and bring joy to others.

Smile until others smile back at you.

I asked her what all this smile stuff was about? She replied, "If you want to develop a meaningful relationship with others, you need to start with yourself first. A smile shows you care, you are compassionate, you are joyful, confident and a smile is contagious."

As my relationship with my mother grew, so did my business. And then life happened.

My mother developed breast cancer and became sick. She insisted I continue to pursue my dream of building my business. Her encouraging smile impacted my life relationships deeply.

T – Transformation to Mindset

Transformation is a powerful word that impacts us in different areas of our lives – physically, personally, and professionally. Transformation begins with our mindset.

I have had many transformations along the way, struggling with finances, confidence, and abilities. Each one opening my thought process to another level of a growth mindset taking me from zero to hero.

As my mother began losing her battle to breast cancer, her bravery and mindset of transformation were changing before my very eyes.

I stayed in her hospital room, bringing my computer so I could keep writing, as she insisted I do. She would smile and ask me about my daily progress. What had I accomplished that day, and how would I help others achieve their goals?

What would it take to facilitate transformation? I thought about my mother. She was my first coach. I realized then, I needed coaching to truly transform myself to achieve massive success in my business, and I continue to do so to this day.

Y – You and Your Why

You have a choice to live your life, your Why, any way you choose. But more importantly, you need to celebrate the amazing opportunities that lie before you.

Why? Because my mother's smile said so. Now it's our turn to PARTY!

It's also okay to be sad; we all are sometimes.

It is difficult for me to write about this personal part of my life because it is the last lesson my mother taught me. As my mother lay in the hospital bed for the last four days of her life, it was a time of reflection for me. Wondering about the power of why we do what we do and share the lessons we learn.

Overcome with sadness, our family gathered around her: my husband Ray, son David, daughter Sherry Rose who is named after my mother and has her smile that lights up a room, and my best friend Laureen.

In those last days, we let my always smiling mother pass with peace and joy. We told stories and laughed so she would feel happy in her final moments, still smiling.

As she slowly took her last breath, I saw that final smile on her face. As if to say, "Keep on smiling, I love you."

My mother, my life coach, taught me about transformation through coaching. I, too, have become a music business coach, and I am passionate about helping you take it to the next level.

The Magic of a Smile and my mother's 5 Powerful PARTY Lessons are my gift to you.

P - What Process Plan do you need to succeed in achieving your goals?

A - What Attitude changes do you need to develop a Positive Mental Attitude?

R - What Relationships do you need to impact those you want to serve?

T - What Transformation do you need to discover gratitude and a growth mindset?

Y - What's your Why and how can you create the greatest PARTY ever?

ACKNOWLEDGMENTS

I want to thank all the musicians for being willing to share their ideas, their expertise, and ultimately their stories of inspiration, and most importantly their Why.

Their Why became the strategies that led them to their success. I am grateful to them and proud to share the *Power of Why* their goals became a reality in this book.

I want to thank my 'UMT Dream Team' Shelagh McKibbon-U'Ren, Joanne Barker, Migelie Luna, and Julie-Kristin Hardt who helped me to implement these ideas and share them with the world.

Thank you to the hundreds of musicians, entrepreneurs, teachers, and students that I have learned from throughout the years, who gave me the framework to build my company, write the *Ultimate Music Theory Program*, UMT Courses, UMT Membership, and compile the *Power of Why - Musicians* Series.

Thank you to our editors Wendy H. Jones and Lisa McGrath for their guidance, expertise, and countless hours in making this book possible.

It is with gratitude to everyone who has taken the risk to dream big and follow their heart to become a musician, an entrepreneur, and generously leave their legacy by enriching lives through music education.

ABOUT THE AUTHOR

ABOUT THE AUTHOR

Glory St. Germain ARCT RMT MYCC UMTC is the Founder/Author 50+ Book of the *Ultimate Music Theory Program* and Founder of the *Magic of Music Movement*. She is on a mission to help 1 million teachers create a legacy through their businesses. She is the host of the *Global Music Teachers Summits*, *Course Creator, Expert Music Teachers Coach, Publisher of the Ultimate Music Theory Series*, and an International Bestselling Author in *The Power of Why* Series, an anthology of global authors.

She is the founder of the *UMTC ELITE EDUCATOR PROGRAM* - A Business Accelerator in knowledge and expert strategies for teachers to use to run successful music studios. She empowers educators to elevate their income, impact their teaching, and build their expert music business while enjoying personal time for self-care, family, and pursuing other passions.

In addition, Glory is an NLP Practitioner (Neuro-Linguistic Programming) and has taught piano, theory, and music for young children for over twenty years. She has served in various leadership positions to support music education organizations.

Glory has spoken on many international stages presenting workshops and is passionate about enriching lives through music education.

Glory loves learning and especially loves books on business and psychology. Mindset is a subject she believes has the potential to change our outcomes. Mindset is limited only by our own thinking. She is a Positive Mental Attitude Advocate and strongly believes that we need to see mindset as a priority, not only for ourselves but also for how we help others think, learn and grow.

She is married to Ray St. Germain, a professional multi-award-winning entertainer and Canadian Country Music Hall of Fame inductee. They have five musically talented children, many grandchildren, and the family continues to grow.

Glory lives her life with gratitude, passion, and serving others through her work.

https://UltimateMusicTheory.com

ALSO BY GLORY ST. GERMAIN

The Power of Why: Why 21 Musicians Created a Program: And Why
You Should Too.

Made in the USA
Coppell, TX
15 August 2021

60537829R10069